County Clare

Tasha Sheipline

Tasha L Sheipline

To my beautiful sister, Tarra.

You are such a kind and patient soul. Mom should definitely live with you when she gets older.

Dear Reader

Dear Reader,

As a writer, music has always played a vital role in providing inspiration for the stories I tell. Songs not only stir the soul, but capture the spirit of the characters as they grow. Below you will find a list of songs that helped to spark my creativity and bring this book to life.

"Lover" Taylor Swift

"Chaconne, Partita No. 2 in D minor" Johann Sebastian Bach

"Valentine's Day" Steve Earle

"Somewhere Only We Know" Keane

Contents

Seanchaí

Throughout the annals of Irish history, the seanchaí have played an important role in the preservation of the culture through oral tradition. In Celtic times, the seanchaí was a clerk of sorts to tribal chieftains, keepers of important information for the clan. Over time, both their role and their stories evolved. No longer were the seanchaí tied to a specific place, becoming free to roam into neighboring communities. The knowledge they possessed began to take the shape of the traditional folklore we see today, as events and experiences derived from those they encountered along the way.

With the infusion of humor, meaningful message, and a deep abiding sense for adherence to history, these storytellers have preserved the national culture through a unique and vivid lens.

Chapter One

BOSTON 1961 - APRIL

Kate McCarthy pulled tight on the front of her wool cardigan, wrapping it around her in an effort to block out the crisp April breeze. The line inched along, testing her already weakened patience. It was opening day at Fenway Park. Apparently, the Red Sox were set to match up against some team from Kansas, but she cared little. Sport was never her thing. All she knew was one side had a ball, and the other team wanted it. The end.

This had all been Patrick's idea, and she was just along for the ride. Some would say she had the tendency to be directionless at times. That was something of a falsehood, for she followed her heart in any direction it should beckon. Up to this point, at twenty-four years of age, she had managed to settle on nothing for any length of time.

Thus far, life had not worked out as planned for her. Born and raised in Boston, she was the daughter of one of the top executives for the Waltham Watch Company. Her father's job provided her with a comfortable upbringing, affording her the opportunity to attend Boston University after graduating high school. To her credit, she managed to last two years before she walked out of the campus gates one day, and, quite simply, never returned. The timing could not have been worse. Her parents' disappointment was compounded when the watch company sold, leaving the family in an all-out crisis.

It took a while but things did turn around. Her father started work at a new company, and Kate picked up a part-time job as a receptionist for a law firm. It was there she met Patrick, the son of one of the firm's partners. Like herself, he hailed from a successful family with a strong Irish background, something that won her parents' approval right away. In their defense, the last few years had been nothing more than a string of disastrous relationships for Kate, each guy less impressive than the next. Given her track record of poor choices, her family couldn't have been more elated to see her land a lawyer's son. After all of their worry, giving this liaison a proper chance was something she knew she owed to them. It was the first time she hadn't seen her dad's eye twitch when she brought someone home. To her, Patrick had the appeal of a bowl of bran flakes with dry wheat toast on the side. He was predictable and monotonous, from his neatly pressed trousers to his argyle sweaters. Not to mention, he had the habit of being clingy, like a stifling wool sweater that had shrunk two sizes too small.

In all honesty, if given the choice, she would have ducked out after their first date. Little aroused excitement in him, and with her being the opposite, it did not bode well for a harmonious coupling. She did her best to make it work, if only to please her parents. After all she'd put them through, she owed them that much. However, as she would soon find out, her bored compliance was one-sided.

At times, she wondered why he stayed with her. It wasn't as if they had much in common. She always had a passion for the arts. In her spare time, she dabbled in music, toyed with writing, and always had a sketchbook tucked away in her bag. But she also possessed the attention span of a gnat, and though she gravitated to many creative pursuits, she had yet to become accomplished at anything thus far. She was a perpetual storm of indecision, while Patrick planned everything in his life with precise detail. For him, an evening at leisure was spent reviewing old litigation cases and the riveting splendor of Massachusetts Revised Code. He was as boring as a college lecture on the mating practices of termites.

Tickets in hand, he flashed her a dazzling-white smile, one that reminded her of the man on the tooth powder advertisement plastered on the wall in the local grocery store. Patrick's white V-neck sweater, outlined in forest green, made him look far too stuffy for the likes of the other working-class men out to enjoy an afternoon at a gritty baseball game. His sandy-blond hair was parted in its signature precision, with not a strand daring to fall out of place. Groaning inside, she trailed behind him as he climbed up the stairs to their seats. The wind gave a solid whip and she reached down, fighting to keep the hem of her dress in place, regretting wearing the stupid thing—far from appropriate attire for the game. Usually, on her day off, she opted for the comfort of a pair of denim pants and a soft cozy sweater, a bit of rebellion against the formality of the professional garb she was expected to wear every day to work. For some reason, Patrick had insisted this was a day that called for something a bit dressier. Clearly, he knew as much about sports as she did.

When they arrived at their seats, she flopped down like a spoiled teenager with an attitude, tucking her billowing skirt between her legs in an effort not to give the rest of the stadium a show, and to retain some fragment of body heat. It was a nice spring day, around fifty degrees, but still far too cool, with the wind swirling up the aisles, to be comfortable in the thin yellow cotton. She pulled the pale-blue headband tighter against her long red curls, then repositioned one of the stray hairpins that had shimmied loose back into place. While she never thought herself a pretty girl, for some reason others did. From the pepper of freckles on her cheeks and nose, to the long lashes that framed her green eyes, her father would say she was a natural beauty.

Looking about, she had to admit that these were at least decent seats, even if she cared more about scoring a bag of roasted peanuts from one of the passing vendors than she did the game. Money had never been much of an obstacle for Patrick, and if his career plans to become a partner at the law firm came to fruition, it never would be. She knew life with him would always be... comfortable, and that was the problem.

Whenever she thought about him, all she experienced was numbness—not one iota of sizzle. She wanted someone who made her skin burn. That dashing Heathcliff from Wuthering Heights who brought out the best and the worst in her all at the same time. A man who smelled like leather and sandalwood, not file folders and carbon paper. She wanted someone who consumed her so much in life, she could haunt him after death. Well... maybe that was a bit too gothic, but somewhere along those lines.

Patrick had barely even touched her over the last long tedious year. All she had gotten was oh-so-appropriate hand holding and a quick peck on the cheek now and then. He'd never attempted one move that couldn't be made in front of a packed church on a Sunday morning. No, not one ounce of sizzle.

And because of that, things were drawing to a close between them. They had been for some time now. She was sure he saw the writing on the wall, though he gave no indication. It was all a matter of her working up the courage to disappoint her parents once more. Day by day, she rehearsed how she would break it off. How she would shoulder her mother's anger and her father's quiet retreat into his study. Most of all, she readied herself for the anguish of feeling like the wayward child for a few weeks, until they softened, and realized that their daughter's reckless spirit could never be tamed.

As she sat there, her thoughts had not only returned to those roasted peanuts but now popcorn toyed with her emotions. With the game nearly halfway through, a sudden awareness dawned that the entire stadium had grown eerily silent. She dragged her focus away from her gurgling stomach and realized that Patrick had gotten to his feet and was looking down at her. In fact, the entire stadium was focused on her. Her gaze darted back and forth like a ping pong ball as she tried to gauge what she had done to become the center of attention. Perhaps her stomach was growling louder than she thought.

Then the unthinkable happened. Patrick knelt on one knee and pulled a blue box from his pocket. Tiffany blue.

"Kate McCarthy, will you marry me?" he shouted, loud enough for fishermen on the Boston Harbor to hear.

She sat there, shell shocked, frozen in absolute terror, with every beady eye burning into her flesh like a hot branding iron. Sweat trickled down the small of her back. Then she did the only thing that came naturally—she said exactly what she was thinking:

"No," she replied, her tone flat, "I don't think I want to do that. I don't want to do that at all."

Chapter Two

IRELAND JULY 1961

It was 2 a.m., the witching hour for starving artists and writers. These days, Kate just happened to be both wrapped into one. She slid her pencil across her sketchbook page, the light scrape sending a soothing sensation through her weary bones. Her mind trickled back to that fateful day in Fenway Park, distracting her from the task at hand.

She replayed it in her head, remembering all too well the deathly silence of the crowd, prompted by something the announcer had said, which she hadn't heard, too busy thinking about peanuts and popcorn. Two things were etched in her memory: the sight of Patrick taking to one knee in front of an entire stadium of people, and the sound of the crowd hurling insults when she publicly declined his offer.

Deep down, she was sure she held some affection for Patrick—she just could not bring herself to call it love. She had felt as trapped as a caged mouse in their relationship, staying only to appease her parents, which, in the end, backfired miserably. If she needed an excuse to end things with Patrick, a public humiliation at Fenway Park did the trick. Within two days, she, Kate McCarthy, found herself the most unpopular woman in Boston, and Patrick offered no shred of sympathy or understanding. His professed love proved far more fleeting than she'd expected. In the blink of an eye, he all but forgot her name. Her only solace was knowing that a lifetime of being married to a man with the personality of a cardboard box would have been worse than this momentary social speedbump.

But things got worse for her. It was the last straw for her long-suffering parents, who were beyond jaded with their daughter's constant indecision. The harsh words between them still echoed in her mind, and their once-loving relationship felt fractured beyond repair. Before she knew it, her bags were packed and a plane ticket was placed in her hand. She was packaged up like a parcel and shipped off, across the ocean, to the care of one of her father's relatives in Ireland. Even if her parents had assured her that her "break" from the city was for her own good, she was no fool; she had become the family embarrassment.

As she thought about recent events, it was clear that her days of absolute freedom needed to come to an end. Now, the time had arrived to start thinking about her future, in a responsible way. Life as an almost-starving artist was beginning to wear her down.

Though she always fought against the constraints that came with security, part of her now longed for something more comfortable. Safe.

She scratched at the spiral-bound page with the charcoal pencil. Art had always been her release from any troubles that saw fit to take refuge in her head. She smiled to herself as she studied the rough etching. The familiar rocky crags of the Cliffs of Moher stretched out upon the page, with merciless waves pounding against the ancient sea walls. It was the natural beauty of these towering wonders that became her saving grace when she arrived in Doolin, a tiny map dot of a village in County Clare, Ireland.

Doonagore House was a property owned by one of her father's distant cousins, her uncle Liam. It was an old country estate, situated at the halfway point between the village and the famous cliffs. Built in the late-eighteenth century, it had been in the Kavanagh family for several generations. The house began its days as a moderate-sized residence, evolving through a patchwork of expansions before being converted into a popular inn for tourists visiting the area. Kavanaghs, the adjoining pub, was a local favorite, frequented by many of the village's colorful cast of characters.

The house had a certain appeal to tourists, radiating a sense of quintessential Ireland. The white plaster exterior was topped with a thatched roof on the main structure. Large flower boxes hung below the diamond-pane windows, giving the altogether plain exterior a much-needed splash of color. For Kate, its picturesque setting, coupled with its close proximity to the ruins of Doonagore

Castle and the cliffs, made it an irresistible opportunity, in a less than desirable situation.

She knew nothing about the day-to-day operations of a guesthouse and pub, but was a quick learner, and not afraid of honest work. In truth, she had always been the social sort, warming to people easily. As a result, she never knew a stranger for long, and could strike up a conversation with anyone, anywhere, at any time. One downside to her outgoing nature was that she tended to be more naive about people than she realized. She was plainspoken, and had the habit of assuming that everyone else was much the same.

Liam and Edel Kavanagh had welcomed her with open arms, showering her with the fullness of their hospitality. It was a nice surprise for the newly dubbed black sheep of the family. She was given a small but nicely appointed private room at the rear of the house. It opened up to the back garden, allowing her to come and go as she pleased. What she loved more than anything about Doolin was the fact that it didn't resemble Boston in any way. Here, the ever-present grind of city life was non-existent. No sounds of traffic blurred out the hum of the wind as it swept across the surrounding grassy fields. On a dry day, she could sit in the garden and listen to the waves crashing against the rugged coastline. These were all luxuries she had never experienced, nor would take for granted.

Though she had only been there little more than two months, she'd settled into a comfortable routine. Her schedule alternated between evening shifts, in both the guesthouse and the pub, allowing her ample time to wander through the surrounding areas seeking inspiration for her artistic endeavors. Neither her job, her writing, nor her art promised to provide her with a lucrative, lasting career, but she was happy for the time being. Clarity existed here; some long-lost sense of purpose that had evaded her for all time seemed to have emerged. Even if she had no idea why, something in her gut told her she was meant to be here, in this place and time. She could do nothing else but ride the wave; its true meaning would reveal itself in time.

The clock on the wall told her it was 2:30, even deeper into the witching hour, and yet she felt no fatigue, used to her new routine by now. She slid back the chair from her small wooden writing desk and pulled the tattered old plaid shawl her mother had given her from the back of the chair. It had been a simple gift from her father to her mother long ago. Now, the once-thick wool was almost threadbare after years of treasured use. She pulled it snug over her ivory-colored sweater, then brushed pencil dust from the leg of her cropped denim trousers. Attire was something she rarely worried about now with her new preference for simplicity. She'd only packed two dresses for her journey to Ireland, leaving all her finest clothing hanging in the closet back home—one last passive dig at her mother.

She flicked on the table lamp by the window. Her trusty flashlight was a requirement, so she grabbed it from the dresser's drawer, then eased the door open, trying her best to soften the loud creak of its old hinges.

The cool night air held a salty tinge that was so inviting she couldn't help but pull it deep into her lungs. Once beyond the garden, she set out onto the narrow path that wound its way through the open countryside in the direction of the great cliffs. Had she not traveled this way many times before at this time, she might have been deterred. With no blazing lights of the city to defuse the night sky, her path was lit with only her humble flashlight, the pale crescent moon, and a blanket of brilliant stars, just enough to keep her footing steady on the well-traveled pathway. Now and again, a stray cloud would wrap the moon in a haze, adding to the mystery of the night.

A diaphanous mist laced the surrounding landscape, the sky hanging like a plush velvet drape, dripping with the finest of glittering jewels. All was quiet, apart from the muffled sound of waves crashing against the sheer cliffs below. She stood tall, towering above them, with hundreds of feet separating her from the icy depths of the Atlantic.

Ireland was a magical place, by day and night. A land so rich in beauty that the shadow of darkness could not diminish its splendor, illuminating the things that could be missed in the light of day, piquing all her senses at once. This place possessed an untamed spirit—timeless, and unchanging. Her life seemed to be an endless search for something, and she was never content with the status quo for any length of time, yet here she found herself at peace.

Every few nights, she walked this solitary route, which took her far away from the jumbled thoughts of daylight. Out here, the world was enormous, yet also tiny. She found herself more and more content with being alone, accepting that she was the only person who truly understood herself.

She moved along, her pace slow, focusing on each step. Now and again, grass brushed against her ankles, encouraging her to shift her position back onto the path. Out here in the darkness, even with the torch, it would be easy to stray off course.

After a while, she stopped, taking time to soak in the splendor that lay beyond the cliff's sharp drop. The ocean was alive, its furious pounding against the rocks below unhindered by the night's coat of darkness. Something about the sea always sparked her imagination. It was so infinite, with no real end or beginning, full of mysteries yet to be revealed. These nocturnal wanderings provided a sense of connection to nature's bounty. To her, the physical world was so entwined with the spiritual sphere, there hardly seemed a difference. Every rock, tree, and sliver of moonlight had its own spirit—a soul that no amount of destruction could extinguish.

As content as she felt here, the gravity of her situation was never far from her mind. What did the future hold for her? Tonight, the bitter sting of her loneliness seemed especially raw, but while she may be somewhat melancholic, she had to admit that, even in the dead of night, these were among the most breathtaking views in all of Ireland. She moved along what had now become a rocky path, with no real destination in mind. The cold mist lingered, layering the crescent moon's façade against the shimmering blackness. Just to be out in these unique conditions made her forget time, or even making it back to bed anytime soon.

This was her usual spot for turning back, but something about tonight felt different, and she willed herself to go on a bit further. Even with her torch, walking this part of the track was dangerous, but she wasn't opposed to a little risk. Being adventurous had always been in her nature—something that wasn't passed down through her family line. Her mother was a guarded and private person, never prone to stepping too far outside the lines of safety, rearing her daughter in a secure home, always shielded from danger and risk as a child. But now, that daughter was a woman, who sometimes found herself gravitating toward peril with careless haste.

When the length of her day began to settle in her weary legs, she decided she'd had enough. As she turned on her heels, the gravel shifted beneath her feet, and the earth shuddered. She stopped dead, aware of the sound of loose stones being tossed about nearby.

Just then, in the inky shadows of darkness, one—no, two figures appeared. The rumbling of stones had stopped but the fresh silence was broken by an audible grunt, sending such a fright through her that she stumbled, losing her footing against the uneven trail. She landed square on her backside, her legs a tangle of rushes, with a sharp pain radiating from her ankle. Her flashlight had tumbled to the ground with her, and now rolled down the small hill, its beam waving about before it disappeared, leaving her in complete darkness.

"What the hell!" a man called out in the gloom, his voice deep.

Chapter Three

Kate barely had a moment to realize what happened when a horse snorted, its hooves stamping on the rocky trail. The clouds shifted enough to release a sliver of moonlight, enough to illuminate the looming presence above – a man, seated squarely on the back of a midnight-black horse. What the hell, indeed.

From her newfound position on the ground, he looked large and imposing. She shuddered, aware that she was scared, and that alone bewildered her as much as what just transpired. It was rare she had occasion to be scared. Most everything she encountered, with proper analysis, could be explained. Yet, here she was, a foolish girl, alone on a dark and dangerous trail – a stretch of land treacherous even in the light of day. She had done a great many stupid things in her life, but this was probably one of her finer blunders. Then again, she did not expect to come across a man on horseback in the dead of night. Still, her habit of venturing out at such a late hour was beyond unwise. Not a soul knew she was gone.

Her eyes widened when the shadowy figure leapt from the back of the horse, his riding boots hitting the ground with a sharp thud. Within a beat, his broad form lurched toward her like some spectral monster in a low-budget horror movie. For a shred of a second, she cowered like a frightened damsel, which annoyed her, because she always hated the predictability of such a role—the weak sniveling female, too scared to give the creature a proper bop on the head. She considered springing to her feet and bolting at lightning speed down the path, but that idea shattered beneath the throbbing pain in her ankle. Without a word, she ran her hands over the ground around her, hell bent on finding anything she could use to wallop against his jaw, but all she came up with were handfuls of meadow grass.

"Just capital, Kate," she muttered under her breath. Unless he had some life-threatening allergy to grass, she could scratch that as an effective weapon.

With a quick pivot, he pulled up and stepped back to his horse. Kate watched, feeling the burn of the dark beast's stare, eyeing her from its position on the high ground.

The man unfastened something from the side of the saddle, then fumbled around until the unmistakable strike of a match preceded a flare of light. Her mouth fell open when she realized he was lighting a small lantern.

He turned back to her and set it on the ground at her feet. In the pale light, he looked at her in such a peculiar way that it caught her breath. It was as though she were someone he had searched the world over to find, and for a moment she blinked at him, wondering if she might know him. That was impossible because, for all the time she'd spent in Ireland so far, she had never seen a man quite like this one.

The light, though weak, was sufficient to show him cloaked in a dark-gray traveling coat, something that looked like it was plucked from a Victorian-era stage production. Its color looked so drab, it matched the melancholy sky to perfection. His linen shirt was unbuttoned at his neck, its loose fabric fluttering in the light breeze. Dampened locks of shoulder-length hair, possibly blond, played against the contours of his face. She changed her mind about the low-budget monster. Now her all-too-vivid imagination painted him like some brooding stranger in a Bronte novel. She stared up at him in silence, almost expecting him to vanish into thin air—a phantom—a mere figment of her wild imagination. Mr. Rochester in the flesh. She liked the sound of that far better than some grotesque creature. Anyway, she would rather be Jane Eyre, the woman far smarter than some sniveling trollop about to be carted off by a swamp fiend.

As she peered through mist-dampened lashes, the lantern's dim under glow lit him up in an ominous way, but her pride wouldn't allow her to show fear. She stiffened her spine, pushing all her initial jitters deep into the background. Whatever his intentions, she was not about to sit there like prey. Over the next few seconds, as they traded looks, all her nervousness faded away. She had always relied on her gut feeling around danger, her intuition proving useful in such situations. Strange as it might seem, there was nothing about this man that made her feel as though she were in harm's way.

"Here, let me help you," he said, as if having read her thoughts, his voice as deep as before. He extended his arm, hand open.

She hesitated, still somewhat unsure. However, she had little choice in the matter when he clasped her forearm, his touch warm, and before she knew it, she was pulled from her grassy cushion.

He steadied her on her feet, watching as she shifted her weight onto her good foot. In her struggle for balance, she leaned against his arm for support, pressing muscles so firm she couldn't help but give an extra squeeze, just to prove he was real.

"You're hurt," he said, letting out a hard sigh.

Her brow tightened as she frowned. Was he making it sound like he was the one inconvenienced? Where is that grass? This bastard will be sneezing for a week.

"I-I am okay," she insisted, well aware they both knew it to be untrue. She placed her heel down, endeavoring to bear more weight on it, but flinched from the resulting pain. "See, all good here," she said through clenched teeth.

"Is it just your foot, then?" he asked, crouching before her, retaining his grip on her arm.

She stiffened as his free hand grazed her lower leg, and struggled not to squirm at the tickling sensation of his touch. Even with a lantern, she was sure he couldn't see much. As it was, she could barely make out the finer details of his features. The softness of his touch sent a slow burn through her, like a shot of really good whiskey. Had it not come at the cost of her pride, she might have considered faking a worse injury just to let him pass over her once more.

"Just my foot," she assured, waving him off. "It really is not so bad. Just let me catch my breath and I will be alright. Really."

He straightened, but caught her arm with both hands when she stumbled forward. Her instability had far less to do with her injured foot and more to do with the heat of his hands rendering her as strong as a house built with mashed potatoes. She silently berated herself. Over the period of just a few minutes, she had managed to become every imaginable cliché version of the delicate femininity she'd avoided her entire adult life.

"Were you coming from that direction?" he asked, nodding to the pathway behind her.

She hesitated, not sure how much to reveal to some unknown person in the dead of night. On weighing her predicament, she accepted that she had little choice.

"Yes. I'm staying at Doonagore House."

He stared off, as if assessing the distance. "That's too far for you to walk on your own." He glanced at the waiting horse, then back at her. "You can't risk more injury to that foot. You will have to ride with me."

"On...the horse?" she sputtered, then pulled herself together. Kate, you imbecile. As if he could have meant any other way.

"On the horse," he echoed, his tone almost fatherly, which made her recoil a bit. Confirmation that he indeed thought he had stumbled upon an idiot. Out here walking in the wee hours of the night.

He probably thought someone forgot to lock up the village nutter after hours.

It made sense that her silly night-time ventures would one day lead her to something like this. For some reason, she had never found common sense to be a necessity, rather a suggestion. Rules of any sort didn't apply to the likes of her.

"I don't know how to ride a horse," she blurted. Her voice was so racked with panic, he looked taken aback for a second.

"The horse knows what to do."

He let go of one of her arms, shifted back, and caught hold of the reins, urging the horse closer until they were both staring into its big black eyes.

"Would you mind giving this injured lady a lift, old friend?"

The horse responded with a quick flick of its head.

"My friend doesn't mind," the stranger said, his tone flat.

Kate wrenched her arm from his grasp and hobbled back a step. "Are you smirking at me? I can't see you, but I know you are smirking at me."

She turned back to the path and began marching away, but her steps were far more difficult than she'd hoped, diminishing the dramatic effect altogether. After a couple of painful yards, she resorted to dragging the foot behind her, soon feeling like the Hunchback of Notre Dame. She'd only traveled a short distance before she decided that was an even stupider plan. It hurt like bloody hell.

"Thank you just the same," she called back, "but I will walk on my own if you don't mind." She switched up her pace again and shifted to a mild hobble. Even though she was sure she now looked like some peg-legged pirate, it proved to be the best option so far.

She managed to get a few yards further when the soft patter of hooves caught her attention.

"Suit yourself. We will just walk along behind you. We weren't quite done with our evening stroll."

Evening? His nonchalant tone grated on her nerves, and she stopped, partly because she wanted to give him a proper scowl, and because she already needed to catch her breath.

"It's probably after three a.m.," she snapped, trying to sound exasperated rather than winded. "Hardly an evening stroll."

"Three a.m. is the afternoon for me," he replied, perched high in his ebony equine tower.

She regarded him for a long moment. "Are you really going to follow me all the way back?"

"I am not going to leave you," he said, sterner now. He patted the horse's neck. "The offer still stands."

She grumbled under her breath, looking down the path. It was so far away, she couldn't distinguish which of the lights flickering in the distance was Doonagore House. She groaned inside, closing her eyes against the inevitable. "Well...I suppose it would be much quicker...and it is getting late."

Without a word, he slid out of the saddle and brought the horse closer, until it stood at her side. Heat radiated from the massive animal, and her nose twitched, filled with an unfamiliar scent, one she could only describe as power and earth intertwined. She blinked, marveling at the sheer size of the beast. It was so much bigger than she'd first thought, its back alone nearly level with the top of her head. Unsure of what she should do, she looked at the waiting stranger.

"I'm going to lift you up into the saddle," he said, his voice soft, as if asking for her permission.

Heat flushed her cheeks at the thought of him trying to hoist her up. While she wasn't what some would call ample, she wasn't bone-thin either. Her physique lay somewhere in-between and, like most women, was still a source of insecurity, never meeting the idea of perfection prescribed by society. She swallowed her momentary need to pass judgment on herself. Surely, this situation was as uncomfortable for him as it was for her. Neither of them could have imagined such a scene would unfold.

She gave a nod of agreement and braced herself against his arm. In one effortless swoop, he lifted her by the waist and planted her at the front of the saddle. Just as she had balanced herself on the beast's back, she almost yelped with the sudden pressure of his body against her back, his presence causing her to go rigid. For some reason, when he said they would ride together, she hadn't considered they would be leaning against one another, touching the whole time. Not that it didn't make perfect sense—she just hadn't thought it through.

He looped his arms under hers and took hold of the reins with one hand, bracing her waist with his other. She'd had her share of uncomfortable moments over the past twenty-four years, but this topped them all. He pulled the lantern from the side of the saddle and thrust it forward for her to hold. After a bit of embarrassed bumbling around, she managed to hold it up, away from the horse's head, not sure the faint light would be of any use to them.

"This will be faster than me leading the horse on foot," he explained, no doubt aware that her body was as inflexible as a steel girder. The only time she'd ever ridden a horse had been as a child at the county fair. As he steered the animal along the narrow pathway at a steady walk, it became obvious that he was accomplished in his skills.

"What are you doing out here at such an hour?" She was far too curious not to ask.

"I was about to ask you the very same thing," he said, chuckling. "I have never been blessed with good sleeping habits. I find the night is my favorite time to ride. Clears the mind."

"I'm not very good at sleeping either," she admitted. "I like the solitude out here."

"While I couldn't agree more, it's still a rather poor choice for us both. These lands can be unforgiving."

"I see that now."

"Somehow, I get the sense that this incident will not deter you from coming out here again."

"You are very perceptive, sir."

He chuckled again, this one conveying real amusement.

They continued on at a slow pace, his warm breath caressing her ear, sending tiny shivers down her neck. For a moment, she felt as if she were wedged between the pages of some cliché romance novel, the type you might find on a dime store shelf. The kind she would have read cover to cover, then went back and did the good parts again.

The muscles in her back wrenched from trying to hold herself upright and maintain some sort of acceptable space between them, without success. However, with the horse's strong but gentle rhythm, she found herself relaxing a little more. This man had an incredible scent—a touch of leather mixed with the earthy warmth of burning peat. It was like being wrapped in a warm blanket on a lazy winter's day. She drank it in, taking slow deep breaths and savoring each one a little longer than the last. The world had somehow faded to black, and she became aware of a strange sensation, faint at first, like a low vibration, but growing to a steady lurch, webbing itself out to every part of her body that met his. A tingle, or...a sizzle.

She had waited her entire life to feel that sizzle, and for no other reason but to experience even more of it, she couldn't deny the urge to shrink back into him a touch more. For a second, she fancied herself as one of those fainting girls, just to have a solid excuse to lean into him without him catching on to her real intentions. It surprised her that, normally dismissive of such fancies, this time she didn't loathe the idea. Anyway, she could blame it on the horse's movement, forcing them so close. She released a silent breath and melted against his solid form, conforming to the peaks and valleys of his chest and abdomen. Even with his arms around her waist, she did not feel restricted, savoring instead a peculiar sense of freedom. She could move away from him anytime she wanted, inching forward to create as much space as her heart desired. But that was the last thing she wanted to do. She rather liked the sensation of being pressed against this alluring stranger.

As they progressed along the trail, she caught sight of something etched into the edge of the saddle. She lowered the lantern and studied the curves of the letters.

"Finnley," she said aloud, her voice muffled by a sudden crash of waves against the rocks below.

"What's that?" he asked, his breath threading through her locks.

"Your saddle, it says Finnley. Is that your name?"

He released a subtle grunt, tightening his grip on her waist as he guided the horse around a curve in the path.

She was unsure if that grunt meant yes. Maybe it was the horse's name. His silence only deepened her curiosity, and she pressed on. "I suppose if your name is Finnley, you go by Finn for short. Like Huckleberry Finn, or Finn McCool." She giggled.

"Not familiar with the Huckleberry lad, but I will take Finn McCool. He outsmarted the Scots, you know."

"My name is Katherine, but I go by Kate. Kate McCarthy."

His chest swelled against her back, as if he were breathing in her name.

"That's a fine Irish name, Miss McCarthy, but I don't get the sense that you're an Irish girl."

She supposed her accent was a dead giveaway. "I'm Irish by blood, on both sides of my family. American by birth."

"What brings you to the likes of County Clare?"

"Cast out of my homeland," she said, flat as could be. "All in all, I suppose I could have been sent somewhere far worse than here."

"Well, I dare say we have that in common, Miss McCarthy."

As she was about to ask him what he meant, a light flickered beyond the hill's ridge. She held up the lantern and motioned toward the dark mass of Doonagore House, lit only by the small lamp she had left at the window, burning through the pitch black of night.

"I'm just over there."

Finn, her gallant knight, pulled up short, as though it would be improper to venture any closer. He maneuvered himself off the horse, then reached up and gripped her waist. Not really knowing the proper way to dismount with an injured ankle, she squirmed beneath his grip, hindering his efforts more than helping. With some wrangling, he lifted her off and placed her on the ground, maintaining his hold on her waist.

"Can you make it back from here?"

"Yes. Absolutely. I will be fine. Really." The walk would take her a minute at full health, two at most with her sore ankle. As she held the lantern up to hand it back, she caught full sight of his face for the first time. The man was almost too radiant for words.

"I-I..." she stammered, not knowing quite what to say.

He released his hold on her and took the lantern, lowering it, his face shielded once again from sight.

"Never mind," she said, shaking her head. "Thank you for the twisted ankle and the ride back on the horse. That really put a spin on my night."

She was thankful for the darkness. By now, Finn was probably convinced she had been expelled from her home country as queen of the idiots.

"I hope to see you again, Kate McCarthy, under better circumstances. You sound...beautiful."

Like something straight out of a dream, he was up on his horse and turning back toward the trail. She stood there, spellbound, watching his form merge with the night.

Chapter Four

Kate awoke the next morning, well past eleven, which was still a tad earlier than usual. She rolled onto her back, shaking off the heavy fog of sleep. Just as she moved her leg, she grimaced as a sharp pain gripped her ankle. She had nearly forgotten. Somehow, she'd thought it was all a dream. She blinked, pushing back the coils of feral hair slung about her face and neck.

Melting into the plushness of her pillow, she stared up at the cracks in the white ceiling, her warm blanket nestling under her chin. Finn's image was still hazy, no doubt because she only got one decent look at him, with the cloak of night keeping him hidden through their encounter. But it mattered little in the light of morning. In fact, it made him all the more intriguing, piquing her interest far more than it should have. She recalled the way the pale glow of the lantern played upon the dreamy curves of his high cheekbones.

"God, no!" she spat out, slapping her cheek. The force of the self-inflicted blow was more than she'd intended, and she rubbed at the resulting heat. That was a bad habit she needed to break.

"Good gracious, no," she said, softer this time, not feeling the need to hit herself again. All the reasons she was here in Ireland flooded back, knocking her senses into check. She knew all too well how much of an utter failure at love she was. The whole of Boston knew it. If she so much as dared think of a man in such a way, she was sure to muck it up. Already exiled from home, she couldn't afford to mess up again, having run out of places to be shipped off to. She only had so many relatives left. Continuing to dream of some nighttime rider who managed to twist her ankle was out of the question. For as long as she lived, she would avoid men at all costs. She would don a nun's habit if she had to. That evoked a grimace. Hmm, maybe not.

Apart from her time with Patrick, and her parents, she had always been known to be brutally honest, rarely afraid to rip the band-aid off someone else's emotional wounds. When her best friend, Adelia, fretted about leaving Boston for a summer in England, she was more than willing to give her a much-needed push. That willingness didn't always pertain to herself but, now her entire world had come crashing down in one swoop, things were different. She would always be plagued with an air of discontent—it was a part of her nature that just couldn't be changed, being headstrong and impossible at times—yet, somewhere along the lines, her fierce resilience had weakened. She was afraid of another failure, and terrified of letting anyone too close. Her heart was like the innermost chamber of a castle, protected by thick stone and layer upon layer of high walls. The more self-doubt weakened her, the more she found another area to fortify.

She was angry at Patrick, and at her parents, but most of all at herself. There was no way to escape the fact that she had never been happy with that man. In truth, she'd strung him along, not just to make everyone else happy but to fill some void she didn't want to face. He'd been good enough for the time, but never in her forever plans. All along, she never bothered to consider that his feelings might be different. Being self-centered, she didn't care to consider that the man she had dated for a year was human too. He may have been as riveting as a brown paper bag, but she didn't have the right to take more from him than she could give in return. Anyone with half a heart would have set him free long before, giving him the right to find real love. She could whine all she wanted about the way she was treated after that day at Fenway Park, but she was not the real victim.

As she slipped out of bed, she spotted the stack of messages on her desk. Nearly each day for the past two months, either her mom or dad had phoned but she'd not accepted even one of their calls. At first, she'd decided that if they needed a break from the shenanigans of their wayward daughter, then her only desire was to give them what they wanted. But her anger had diffused over time, and it was so long since they'd spoken, the sheer awkwardness of their relationship filled her with angst. She was lonely, and she missed them, but she wasn't ready for those first steps yet.

After testing her injured foot, groaning on seeing the dark bruising, she washed up and dressed, then pulled her hair back in its usual ponytail, using a rolled-up headscarf to keep all the loose tendrils in place. She hobbled out the door, a trip to the local chemist at the forefront of her mind. Her throbbing ankle wasn't going to make work an enjoyable experience tonight, with her shift scheduled from five until closing.

She limped out to where her scooter was parked in the gravel drive. It was an older model Ivory-colored Vespa she'd bought soon after arriving, well-worn from years of travel up and down the county roads. Even though it was scratched to high heaven—evidence of its previous owner's lack of good driving—it got her where she needed to go, and cost effectively at that. She pressed the helmet onto her head, tucked up errant strands of hair, and fastened the strap under her chin. With the scooter fired up, she eased out onto the road that would take her the short distance into Doolin.

The village was a beautiful place, even if it was much smaller than her old neighborhood in Boston. Its main line of businesses lay along the one road that snaked through it, with brightly colored buildings attracting the tourists heading for the Cliffs of Moher or a boat to the Aran islands. The village was well known for its pubs, and boasted some of the best traditional musicians nearly every night. What struck her most about this place was that she knew more of the locals than she did the neighbors on her street back home. Such was the way in Ireland. There was an immediate sense of belonging here, brought on by the kindness and hospitality of the people.

After parking along a boreen—a side lane—she knocked the kickstand of her scooter into place with her good foot, then hobbled along the footpath toward the chemist. She'd almost made it to the door when her name was called out from behind.

"Fine day it is, Miss McCarthy, but you don't look like you're doing so well."

She turned to see Aonghas Clune, known as Old Gus by the locals. He was a seanchaí—a storyteller of folklore—and a regular at Kavanagh's. This man spent his years scouring the country, collecting stories from the older generations. Ireland was a mysterious land, its folklore dating back a millennia, long before the stories had ever been written down. As a seanchaí, Old Gus was committed to hearing the stories and preserving them through the same oral traditions passed down through time immemorial. He was a fantastic storyteller, vivacious and colorful, drawing a crowd just about anywhere he went. The Good People were his favorite topic—what Kate had always known as fairies, though she caught on fast that it wasn't a term the locals liked to use. A belief still existed that to call them such could invoke their anger.

Gus was old enough to be her grandfather, but still as sharp as a razorblade. There wasn't a story he couldn't recall, or a detail about a person he didn't pick up on with a quick observation. His years of traveling and collecting the stories of people from every walk of life had endowed him with a kind and gentle disposition, and a rather good appreciation for humor.

A widower, he spent his evenings at the pub, except for Fridays, which he reserved for the sessions. Since arriving in County Clare, Kate had heard all about the Friday-night sessions. Each week, the locals would gather at a different house, where they would share in a large meal composed of traditional recipes that had been passed down through generations. Afterwards, there would be live music played, dancing, and the telling of stories by Old Gus the seanchaí. The party would wear on long into the night—a much-needed reprieve from a solid week of hard work. To date, she had not attended one, but she always got a play-by-play account of each one on Saturday night when Gus returned to the pub.

"I had a bit of a mishap up on the cliff trail last night," she told him, nodding down at her foot. "I'm heading in here to see if I can get something to patch me up before my shift this evening."

"Rightly so," he said, surveying her unsteady stance as she braced herself against the building. "What sort of a mishap did you have?"

"Well, it was about half-two in the morning, and I decided to take a stroll along the cliffs—"

"Who on God's green earth goes out at half past two for a stroll?" he exclaimed, throwing up his hands.

She stared back at him, doing her best not to scowl. "I established that I was an idiot last night. May I continue?"

"Oh, by all means," he answered, waving her on.

"Well, out of nowhere, comes this man on a black horse."

Gus raised his brow at this unexpected nugget.

"So, I was startled, you see, and fell to the ground, and that's how I twisted my ankle."

"There was a man riding a horse along the cliffs at half past two?" He cupped his chin, scratching at the rough bristles as he pondered.

"Yes," she said, almost snarling, though it was more at the pain in her ankle than at Old Gus. "Well, Finnley brought me back home, and...here I am."

"Finnley? That was his name? Finnley?"

"I am pretty sure that was his name, though it might have been the horse's..." She trailed off. Gus was used to far-fetched stories, but she didn't want to continue. The more she spoke, the more she felt like an ignorant American. No doubt, the seanchaí came to that conclusion the first time he'd met her.

"Well, I shouldn't hope to hinder you further. Maisy will fix you up right." With that, he tipped his hat, letting the fine strands of his muddy-gray hair peek out.

Kate nodded, pivoted on her good foot and limped into the chemist's.

Chapter Five

That evening, patched up as good as could be, Kate walked into the pub ready to start her shift, just before the skies opened. It was one of the older sections of Doonagore House, the walls covered with weathered oak paneling that hadn't lost the silky sheen of varnish quite as much as the creaky old floorboards. Pictures of locals past and present hung everywhere. Old black and white stills of men holding up ribbons after a grand win at the sheepdog trials were butted up beside photos of others with a prized catch out at the pier. The hint of decades of peat burned in the old fireplace permeated the air, coupled with the heavy scent of someone's pipe smoke billowing out of the snug in the far corner.

It was still early, with only three tables occupied. Outside, rain pelted down in sheets, and long gone was the fair afternoon she had enjoyed earlier. Around here, the weather changed its mind more than she did.

"We've had all four seasons today," was a popular saying. She gave a fake laugh every time it was uttered, as if she hadn't heard it a hundred times before.

She busied herself, checking stock and drying off glasses. Try as she might, she couldn't forget her encounter with Finnley – her stiff ankle not allowing him to venture far from her thoughts. She couldn't get that face, at least what she could remember of it, out of her mind. Why did he have to be so good looking? It would have been far more convenient had he been short, balding, with a crooked back. That image might be far easier to erase from her mind.

At half past five, Old Gus came in, taking his usual seat. He was clad in his favored forest-green wool sport coat, with a matching flat cap. Though he was a regular, he never partook in spirits, preferring a hot cup of tea with two teaspoons of brown sugar. He could nurse a full kettle's worth the whole night through, sitting back and taking in the delicious conversation around him.

"Grand day for the ducks," Seán Campbell called out as he stepped into the pub, shaking rain off his coat. The sound of the downpour was muffled as the wooden door closed behind him. It was a gray evening, with the promise of rain forecast well into the night.

Seán was a short, squatty man, his mousy-brown hair shattered by slivers of gray strands. A distinguishing detail was his mustache—always overgrown, and in desperate need of a good trim. His wrinkled shirt, tucked at crooked angles into his trousers, gave the impression he got dressed in the dark. He spoke in a loud voice, laughed even louder, and had the habit of being a beat or two behind in every conversation. The man had the knack of being off-putting for some—not everyone's cup of tea. However, he once remarked that she reminded him of Maureen O'Hara. That comment made him a tad more likable in her book, even if just for a moment.

He pulled his hat from his head and gave it a few taps against his palm, spraying raindrops onto the bare floor.

"You got the floor all wet," she scolded, not impressed. "Who's going to clean up that mess?"

"So, I did," he said, scrutinizing his handiwork with pride. It was clear her reprimand had no effect. "I will take a pint, if you please, Miss McCarthy."

She deepened her scowl, but obliged his request, grabbing a glass from the shelf. Gus gave a chuckle from the corner, and she flashed him a fiery glare that silenced him.

Pint in hand, Seán shuffled his way toward Gus, his wet boots squeaking as he walked. It was far louder than it needed to be, and Kate felt sure he was doing it on purpose.

"Where will your travels take you this week?" Seán bellowed out to Old Gus, taking an uninvited seat across the table. He swigged a hearty gulp of the foam-capped liquid from his glass.

"The Byrne house just up the road this Friday," the seanchaí replied.

"Ah, good spot indeed. Mrs. Byrne makes a hell of a good stew." He turned his attention back to Kate, his plump cheeks gleaming over a pleasant smile. "What about you, Miss McCarthy? Will you be joining us for the session this week?"

Busy wiping up the puddle of water on the floor, she wasn't impressed by his wide toothy smile. No doubt his inquiry was just an attempt to smooth over her irritation with him. Though invited to the session most every week, she had never mustered up the courage to go. Being a transplant in Doolin, locally referred to as a 'blow-in,' she'd felt accepted, but still hadn't managed to make any close friends. She would be hard pressed to admit it but the prospect of showing up alone was a little embarrassing. Knowing only a few people, she doubted she would be comfortable enough to enjoy herself.

"I have to work on Saturday," she replied, turning back to the floor. "I don't think it would be wise to be out so late." She stayed clear of the fact that she worked the evening shift, and rarely rolled out of bed till well after noon on any given day.

"Might you consider bringing your newfound suitor?" Old Gus chimed in. "Such a gentleman would surely guarantee you were home at a reasonable hour."

She shot him a reproachful look but continued mopping the floor. Best to say nothing.

"Suitor?" Seán asked several seconds later, his voice lifted. His red face beamed, as if someone had just offered him a huge slice of birthday cake with a hearty dollop of ice cream on the side.

"I told you that in confidence, Gus," Kate snapped.

"Be reasonable, child," he said, his tone soft. "You can't expect a happening as good as this to be kept secret."

"Have you forgotten Old Gus is a seanchaí?" Seán added. "You can't expect a storyteller not to repeat a good story."

Kate glared at the two men, though it did little to dissuade them. They were the town's busybodies, after all.

"What suitor?" Seán asked again, his gaze darting from her to Old Gus.

"Just a lad she stumbled upon last night," Gus answered. "Miss McCarthy, what did you say the lad's name was again?"

"Did I say his name?" she asked, knowing full well she had. "If you must know, his name was Finnley."

She liked the way his name rolled off her tongue.

"Finnley?" Old Gus repeated, slow and steady, each letter given its own time.

"Only Finnley I know is the retired post man," Seán said, wrinkling his nose. He took another sip of his pint. "He must be about eighty now. What on earth do you want with a man old enough to be your granddad?"

"That's not him," Kate growled, looking at him as if he had just grown a horn out of the top of his balding head.

"What did you say your lad's surname was again?" Old Gus leaned forward, like a detective in an interrogation room.

"I didn't actually ask him." She stamped the mop on the floor, never wanting a conversation to end quite so bad. "I just know his name is Finnley, but he goes by Finn. It was late, well past three a.m. by the time I got home. I wasn't thinking clearly. I didn't think to ask for his birth certificate and other official documents.

I twisted my ankle, and he gave me a ride back home on his horse. His name is Finn, and that is all I know."

"Gave you a ride on his horse?" Seán's jowly chin wobbled. "What in the world is a man out riding a horse for in the wee hours of the morning? And what were you doing at that hour?"

The man could barely get the questions out of his mouth fast enough. Kate visualized dust coming off his brain, with it not having worked this hard in a good long while.

"Finnley. That's old Gaelic for a fair-haired hero," Old Gus muttered to himself, and Kate just about caught it. She tried to remember if Finn had fair hair but it didn't come to her, recalling that old turf smell from him instead, or was that from the pub's fireplace?

"Are you about ready for another pint then, Seán?" she asked, knowing full well how easy it was to divert his attention.

"Don't mind if I do," he said before emptying his glass with another deep swig.

She fixed him his second pint, hoping this would shut him up for a bit.

As she limped her way back to the table, pint in hand, Seán glanced down at her foot.

"What's wrong with your foot?"

True to his nature, he was always lagging in his observations and just about every conversation. She surmised that a brain the size of a pea could only process things so fast.

"I told you, I twisted my ankle when I fell. Finnley gave me a ride back here."

"And you're sure that this Finnley isn't the old man who used to bring the post?"

She gave him a vicious scowl, not bothering to answer his question, spun on her good foot, and retreated to the relative safety behind the bar.

"She sure is a feisty one," Seán said. He took another healthy sip. "So tell me a story, Old Gus. Something from up north. I'm heading that way in a few days."

"Any chance you could stay indefinitely?" Kate called out, unable to resist the urge.

"No chance at all, Miss McCarthy. I wouldn't want you to be without your Seán for long. I am just heading to Sligo and then straight back, good Lord willing."

"Sligo," Old Gus said, smiling. "I recall a tale about Sligo. One of the old people told it to me long ago. Let me see if I can remember it." He gave the top of his head a scratch, as if to stimulate his memory. It was out of habit more than anything—the man rarely forgot anything.

"Once in the time of the great blight of the mid-eighteen forties, there was an old farmer. Beholden he was to a greedy landlord, who would take no greater pleasure than kicking him off his lands if he was a day late on his rents. As with many families, the crop had gone bad, and this man was no exception in his fortune. As if anything could get worse, his son and daughter, his only two children, had taken ill. Much to his grief, the son died, leaving the daughter not long to follow. There was no food to nurse her back to life, and all he could do was wait for the inevitable."

Kate leaned her chin on her hand, elbow resting on the bar counter. Old Gus had a way of telling a story that stopped her in her tracks.

"One day, he went out to visit the place where he had buried his son. There, deep in the ancient forest of Slish Wood, he stood weeping at his son's grave, under the roots of a large old Hawthorne tree. Bitterness filled his heart, knowing that soon he would bury his daughter too. It was as if his soul had entered the longest of dark winter nights, so great was his loss. He let out a curse upon the earth, the Good People, and anything else that came to his mind."

"As he turned to walk away, he heard a rash of shouts. Turning to find the source, he stood face to face with a fair-haired man.

"'How dare you curse me,' the man shouted with wildfire in his eyes. 'You have pulled me from my world, and sentenced me to life in yours. You will release me at once.'

"The hollow-eyed farmer looked him up and down. Indeed, his curse had sentenced the fairy to life here in this world, and he could only be released if the farmer willed it to be so. The once-kind and gentle farmer had been hardened so much that he refused.

"'If I am sentenced to this life of misery, then you shall be too. 'Twas you who has brought this misfortune upon my house. It's you who will pay.'

"Furious, the fairy would not relent, stalking the farmer's lands day and night, till one day he came to look in the farmer's window, and there, sick as a woman could be, lay the farmer's daughter. As he looked upon her, all the bitterness in his heart for the farmer disappeared. Something about human love made him realize his heart wasn't complete. The emotions were so strong, he would gladly stay in this realm if only for her to be well again. Over time, the farmer softened, and released the fairy, but he would not go. Never had he experienced love such as this, and he was determined not to return to his world without finding it for himself."

Kate found herself moving from behind the bar, anxious to get close enough to drown out the chatter of the other patrons. There was never a time that a story from Old Gus didn't pique her interest. She had learned a great deal about her new home and surroundings from the way he brought the stories of everyday people to life. Like many of the seanchaí, he had scoured the county and beyond, seeking out the tales of the old people, as he called them. He gravitated toward them, gleaning from their knowledge and experiences, and relishing in the tales passed down to them by their own families. This was the secret to the rich heritage of Ireland—the understanding that these stories helped to paint the picture of real life. They spoke of their trials and tribulations and the hope that resided deep within these difficult times. Old Gus was a master at taking these tales of a bygone era and breathing life into them again. He was a captivating speaker, drawing in anyone who took the time to listen to him.

As she moved to occupy one of the empty stools at the bar, she caught a glimpse of something from the corner of her eye.

"Is that your comb on the floor?" she called out to Seán, pointing to the small wooden object lying where he had stood earlier. It surprised her that she hadn't seen it while mopping his mess.

"What's that you say?" He lowered his glass to the table, froth tracing the line of his overgrown mustache. Old Gus eyed Kate's hand as she bent to pick it up.

"Don't touch it!" the men shouted in unison, causing her to lurch back two steps and nearly tumble. She laid her hand across her heart, trying to quell its wild thump.

"What on earth?" She shot them a look of disbelief.

"Don't ever touch a comb on the floor, girl," Seán barked, his red forehead beaded with perspiration. "Are you daft?"

"Daft?" Her mouth fell open. "Who are you calling daft, you old fool?" She squared her shoulders at him, like a lion readying for the pounce.

"That, right there, is the work of the banshee," he said, pointing a trembling finger as he looked to Old Gus for validation. The seanchaí just stared down at the comb in silence.

"The banshee?" Kate gave an unceremonious roll of her eyes. "You mean to tell me that the banshee sneaks around and sprinkles combs on the floor? What a bunch of nonsense."

"She foretells death, you know. Some hear her cry out into the night. An old woman with a lonesome, mournful wail. Others say she is a young woman, beauty beyond compare, who sits along a lonely road, combing her hair. If you touch that comb, she will come looking for you later, she will."

"What are you talking about, you old goat?" Kate spat. A comb? Of all of the ludicrous notions.

Seán gave her a twisted-up scowl. "On second thought, let the banshee take you." He laughed as he looked at Old Gus, the sound coming as a cackle.

"Well, who's going to pick it up?" she asked, hands on hips. "We can't just leave a comb lying on the floor forever."

Without a word, Old Gus moved to the unlit hearth at the far wall. He held his lower back as he picked up the black iron log grabber. Then, with caution, he walked over to the comb. After a few attempts, he gripped it with the tongs and turned on his heel toward the door. Without prompting, Seán shuffled over and opened the door with a violent pull. Old Gus approached it with a sure and easy tread, and when he reached the threshold, he flung the comb out into the grass beyond the stone steps.

Kate watched in amazement as the two men turned back to her, triumphant. Seán gave her a cheeky grin as he crossed over to his waiting pint. He picked it up and took a loud slurp that almost turned her stomach. True to his nature, Old Gus remained silent as he replaced the log grabber back at the hearth, drawing no attention to himself. A thunder of applause erupted from the other patrons, as though both men had just saved them from certain death. Seán soaked it up, stepping out into the middle of the floor and giving a little bow, while Old Gus just took his seat again.

"No need to thank us for saving the day," Seán chimed, a smug grin lifting his cheeks. "It was the least we could do for ya, my lady."

"I wasn't about to thank you for anything," she said, hobbling back behind the bar. She wasn't ignorant to the superstitious nature of her patrons, but this whole scene felt overdone.

Seán waltzed over to Old Gus. "Next time, I will distract her and you slip the comb in her pocket. The banshee will whisk her away and all of our problems will be solved."

Old Gus gave a muffled laugh, and Kate let out an exaggerated huff. By now her ankle was throbbing, but a glance at the clock on the wall evoked a sigh. Still several hours until the pub closed. She supposed that was her penance for being so stupid. This gnawing pain was a sign to remind her why thinking of Finn was a bad idea. Still, from time to time, as the night wore on, he came to mind. She was in no shape to take her evening stroll along the cliffs later, but she wondered if he would. Would he wander, restless, in the stillness of the night, a swirl of thoughts in his head? Would any of those thoughts be of her?

She shook her head, snapping herself back to reality. Time to focus on her work. She was not going to think about a man. That was the last thing she should be doing. If her mind dared to conjure up some mysterious dreamlike image of him, she would brush it away—tell herself he was just some weird guy stalking along the cliffs at night, and on a giant black horse. He was anything but what she wanted him to be—some hazy manifestation of her imagination.

Her shift stretched out. Though heavy rain was quite normal, and it rarely kept people from going about their routine, things remained slow. It was early July, a time when the weather warred against itself—a clear day, with the sun shining one moment, and pelting rain the next. The days were always unpredictable, not unlike the weather she was accustomed to back along the New

England coast. All one could do was take each day as it came. The weather, much like life, offered little sense of control.

When the pub closed at last, she could not be more relieved. For once, she felt as though she could crawl into her bed and sleep the whole night through. She was far too exhausted to think of much else.

She pulled up a bag of rags used to wipe down the tables. "James, I will drop these off at the laundry door on my way home."

James, one of the other bar keepers that night, nodded, then flicked the overhead lights off, shrouding the empty space in shadows.

As she walked out the front door, she smiled at the fact that the rain had ceased, at least long enough for her to limp the short distance back to her room without getting soaked. James pulled the heavy door closed and locked it as she waited, then he headed off in the opposite direction as she trudged along the cobblestone pathway. The dark sky was cloudy, and her uncle Liam's small ground lights lit her way, gleaming off the stones, still slick from the earlier downpour. She heaved the bag to one side, leaning in the opposite direction to keep her balance.

She scanned the grass surrounding her, not sure where the comb had landed, hoping she'd managed to pass it already. Though not in the least bit superstitious, a tingle ran through her as she thought about the banshee crouching somewhere in the darkness, waiting. She continued on, took a sharp turn at the pub corner, and walked to the laundry door. The stillness of the night made her want to hasten her steps, but her ankle had other ideas.

Just then, something behind her fluttered, and she froze, a looming sense of danger overtaking her desire to escape. The sound came again, and her breath caught. Was it someone moving through the grass, or a wolf sizing up its prey? No, there are no wolves in Ireland anymore. The banshee? Right then, the fringes of her imagination were ablaze, and she could almost feel the long skeletal fingers pawing at her hair.

Just as she was about to succumb to her fate, the city dweller in her surfaced—the woman who was well versed in the avoidance of the dark alleyways and low-lit streets of a Boston night. Her mind shot to the only weapon she had at her disposal, and with a violent thrust, she swung the bag of rags at the source of her angst.

A second after releasing its weight, a thud signaled that it landed against something firm—something unseen, but no less there. It mattered little what it hit, she was already in a steady shamble down the path, eyes fixed on the door to her room just a few steps ahead.

"Well, I suppose that's a twist of fate."

She stopped dead. Even if she couldn't quite place it at first, she knew that voice—its deep resonance swirling through her head. When she turned into the darkness, she couldn't make anything out other than a tumbled mass just off the stone path. Was that the laundry bag, on top of something?

A groan came from it, then it moved, and the laundry bag rolled over. She held her breath through the following silence, but then released it, her sense of doom somehow dissipated, replaced by an oppressive curiosity.

She eased her way, in a sideways gait, back to the laundry-room door. Never so much as taking her focus from the tangled mass on the ground, she found the handle, twisted it, and eased the door in until the hinges creaked, a sound she'd become familiar with. She stepped through, backing up until the chain brushed the crown of her head.

After a firm tug, her world was bathed in a soft golden glow that stretched out through the doorway to the figure on the ground. By now, he was lying back, propped up on his elbows, as if lounging the night away in the wet grass. For the first time, she could behold him in full light. She had never been a good judge of age, but he was clearly older than her, if only by a handful of years. His mid-length golden locks looked tussled, evidence of the calamity he had just endured. She followed the gentle curve of his jaw to the ridge of his high cheekbones, and landed into the depths of the grayest eyes she had ever seen. They reminded her of the melancholy in the world—all of it—and it was like something pricked at her heart. If his eyes betrayed him, she couldn't be sure, for all she saw was the full pout of his lips curved up in a mocking grin.

Then, every bit of willpower dissolved, and she smiled.

Chapter Six

For mere seconds, Kate blinked at the glorious vision facing her, before the reality of what had just transpired fully set in. Then her edges started to sharpen.

"What is wrong with you?" she snapped, her tone hushed to a whisper.

"Me?" he said, his smile fading as he rolled onto his side and pushed himself up with a breathy grunt.

"What are you doing, sneaking up on me in the pitch dark? What are you, freaking Dracula?" For a moment, she wondered if Bram Stoker had ever considered a simple laundry bag as a means to destroy the undead. It had been powerful enough to knock Finn on his ass.

"I walk out here now and then." His effort at nonchalance was unconvincing.

He looked taller than she remembered but, then again, the details of last night were now something of a blur. She curled her lip at him like a feral beast, her heart still thundering, her ankle aching, and pure agitation filling her insides. A sudden urge to unleash all her troubles on him gripped her.

"In the dead of night? Here outside the pub? No, you do not walk out here now and then. I have lived here long enough to be sure that I have never seen the likes of you here."

"You just missed me, then," he retorted. "I have been wandering these parts for a good long time."

"I never saw you." She stepped out of the doorway, shadowing his face with her frame, which she was glad for; the way the light had touched his eyes proved far too distracting. Not good if she wanted to retain her steely resolve.

"Were you looking for me?" His brow raised just before a devilish grin dimpled his cheeks.

A rush of heat pulsed through her, and she struggled to convince herself that it was still anger.

"N-No! Why should I be looking for you? I barely even know you. And the two times I've met you are enough to make me think I shouldn't want to know you at all." She crossed her arms and pouted.

"Yes," he said, nodding in agreement, "I can see how you might come to that conclusion."

"Were you out here looking for me?" she asked, trying not to sound too eager.

"Not after you hurled that bag of whatever straight into my gut."

"Dirty laundry."

"Uuggrrr." His face scrunched up.

"I thought you were the banshee," she said, pushing past him to the heap of rags now spilled out of the bag. She groaned, and bent to snatch them up one by one to shove them back in.

"The banshee?" He looked out into the darkness. "If she were here, she is long gone now. I suppose she has business elsewhere." He brushed against her arm as he moved by her and followed suit, picking up a few rags that had scattered beyond the light.

"You know her personally?" She straightened, giving him a wrinkled-nose grumble – the kind she reserved for the likes of Seán when he sputtered on about all of his hocus pocus. "Have a spot of tea and a fresh-baked scone with her now and then?"

"I know a great many folk."

"Oh? Are all these folk men, then? It is clear to me that you know nothing about women. For if you did, you would know that lurking about in the dark is not exactly flattery. Rather, it is a little alarming. Back where I am from, we call it a nuisance, and we phone the police."

He stared back with a bemused smile that irritated her even more. She glared at him, then reached down to pull the bag up into her arms, realizing that, now the rags had lain in the wet grass, they were heavier than before.

"Allow me," he said, reaching out to relieve her of her burden.

She twisted away, the bag clutched to her chest. "I have it."

"I don't want to stifle your spirit—Irish by blood, American by birth, girl—I just want to carry the bag for you." He stretched out his arms, hesitant, no doubt unsure if she would relent and accept his offer.

She ran her tongue along the inside of her lip, staring at his waiting hands. With a resigned huff, she shifted her weight forward and released the bag, allowing it to roll into his palms.

He responded with a quick smile. "In the door then?"

She closed her eyes for a moment, then led the way to the laundry room, aware that he kept his distance as he followed, her fierce need to retain her independence obviously not lost on him. He did not seem opposed to respecting it, so long as it didn't infringe on his own sense of chivalry. That worked for her, for now.

He plonked the bag onto the old tile floor and stepped back out to wait on the cobblestone path. She pulled the chain, returning them to the shadows of the night, then closed the door behind her.

"Were you hurt?"

He looked at her. "Come again?"

His voice held a startled ring, as if her question had tapped into a space shared with no one else.

"When I hit you with the bag? Were you hurt?"

"Ah, not so much."

"I don't think I would have been all that sorry if you were," she confessed, pushing a loose curl behind her ear. "You knocked me over, after all, last night."

"Do you always say every single thought that comes into your head? Ever have the need to soften the blow a bit?"

"No," she said, twisting her cheek in embarrassment. "It has got me in trouble from time to time."

He nodded once. "This I can see. However, I do apologize for knocking you down last night. You didn't leave the encounter unscathed, and for that I am truly sorry." He nodded at her ankle, then rubbed his abdomen. "Still, I think you have enacted your revenge quite impressively."

"Now that you mention it, I do feel better." She couldn't hold back a sly grin. "Watching you roll on your back like an overturned turtle was remarkably satisfying."

"Well, as fun as it was, you need to rest that foot, and I have a journey home."

She raised a brow, tilting her head. "How far?"

"Cahermann Hill, not too far from here."

The place he named didn't ring a bell. She had explored a great deal of the surrounding areas, but still hadn't managed to become familiar with the whole of County Clare. There were always new places and people to discover here.

She peered into the darkness, looking for his black horse. It was nowhere to be seen. "I'm a good twenty paces away, maybe twenty-two with the bum foot. I suppose I do need to get some rest. I have an early start tomorrow." She failed to mention that, by 'early start,' she meant noon.

"Do you have plans for the day?"

She stiffened, lifting her head. "I have a date tomorrow."

"A date?"

A wisp of something in his tone resembled disappointment. She had no idea why but that brought a surprising sense of delight.

"I have a date with myself. I am going to Glencree to walk the old glen. I want to take in some scenery and then sit and read my book. Alone."

"Alone?"

"And by alone, I mean I want to read my book, and not see your face creeping about."

"What book?"

"It's a collection of Irish folklore by William Butler Yeats. Old Gus gave it to me to read."

"Old Gus? Is that your suitor?"

For a moment, she pondered how on earth he didn't know Old Gus. He was a local legend, for crying out loud. Then again, her gut told her Finn wasn't exactly the social type. He seemed to be a bit on the introverted side, and the hours he kept weren't conducive to getting out and making friends, at least not the normal variety. The man could not be faulted for being shy, but befriending folks such as herself might not be his best option. She wasn't what most would consider all that likeable.

"No, he is not my suitor. What is with all you daft men? Can't a girl just be happily single? What's with the word *suitor*, anyway? Who even uses that word anymore?"

"I suppose you don't have to be attached to be happy," he agreed. "It does get rather lonely, though, doesn't it?"

"No," she shot back. Aware that her voice had gotten loud enough to wake the guests, she brought it right back. "I am perfectly happy keeping men at a comfortable distance. If you have some image of me crying my nights away and taking up a collection of forty-two cats to ease my sorrow, you are vastly mistaken."

"That would be a lot of cats," he mumbled, and she saw that it was more to himself.

"That is a tremendous number of cats. I wouldn't make enough money at work to feed them all. I like cats, don't get me wrong but..." She groaned inside, realizing she'd gone right off track. "Anyway, do not show up at the glen."

"You have my word, fair lady. I won't be at the glen. I shall not bother you, or your book, or the cats."

She stared back, like a bear that had just been poked, but said nothing. A part of her wanted to prolong his stay, even for a short time. She tapped the cobblestone with her bad foot, not sure what to say, but also giving him the chance to move the conversation forward. He didn't take the bait. Was that intentional, or was he as bad at reading women as she thought?

"Goodnight, Kate," he whispered, dipping into a low bow as he stepped back into the shadows. "Until our paths cross again."

She stood there, watching as his dark form dissolved into the night like an ominous specter. Considering the established pattern, who would be the one to get injured the next time their paths crossed?

Within the new silence, loneliness enveloped her. Though she'd done everything in her power to assure him that his presence was not wanted, she had to admit to being a little sad at his departure. This was difficult to puzzle out, what with her feeling flattered and rejected all at once.

A man like Finn normally stood no chance against a perfect storm like her. She would push him away just to be mad at him when he listened. But something told her he was not the pushover she usually attracted. For one thing, he was witty enough to give her back what she doled out. Yes, he piqued her interest, to be sure. Whether or not that was in a good way had yet to be decided. He reminded her of Mr. Darcy from Pride and Prejudice, one of her favorite novels, with his arrogant smirk that roused her irritation, masking the softer side of his nature that appeared now and then. Did that make her Elizabeth Bennet, trying to wrangle in her common sense against the flood of emotions he evoked? Now she thought of it, she had the urge to re-read that book, but like a dating guide this time.

Chapter Seven

It was half past noon when Kate emerged from her lair, a book tucked under her right arm, a folded blanket slung over her left, and holding a small bag of cookies she'd swiped from the welcome table in the inn's lobby. She packed all of her provisions into the basket on the back of the scooter, then took stock. It was her day off, and her ankle felt much better, giving her hope that she might be able to enjoy the excursion unhindered by the limp that had dominated every waking moment since her misadventure on the cliff path. She pulled a small notebook out of the satchel slung across her shoulders. When she first arrived in Doolin, she'd started jotting down all the places she wanted to visit in the county. Each time a location was suggested, she noted it on a new page, adding the directions and rough-sketched maps. She flipped through the pages until she found the one for the old glen, then took a minute to study her notes. With that, she snapped the notebook shut and tucked it away for the ride.

As she got on the scooter, she glanced down at her bare knees and groaned. Her choice of attire was not one of her more thought-out decisions. She pulled at the blue dress's hem and tucked the fabric under her thighs. It would have to do. Once her helmet was fastened, she started out on the day's adventure.

The old glen was a wooded area that bordered a small river with a nice view of quaint falls that proved a main attraction for visitors. Being a weekday, she anticipated it would be quiet, with mostly locals about. The promise of a break away from the hustle and bustle of the pub was like a dream come true. These past few weeks were busier than usual, and she'd not been able to carve out much time for herself. She needed this bit of respite from the world.

Her trip to Glencree consisted of about fifteen minutes cutting through a web of rural roads. It was a clear summer day, the temperature warm, and the breeze just right. Even though there wasn't a cloud in the sky at present, she'd learned the hard way not to trust the weather here, and had tucked a rain slicker into the basket just to be safe.

Twisting trails weaved through the woods, the full canopy shading her from the afternoon sun. As expected, the area wasn't too busy with tourists, and she walked along, enjoying the birdsong and the hum of bugs. With this being her long-awaited escape from everyone and everything, she had built it up in her mind. The old glen was the quiet retreat she'd been wanting, but now she was here, she felt somewhat underwhelmed. Being out here alone was... well, in a word... boring.

Each time she caught sight of an unfamiliar face, disappoint-ment fluttered low in her chest. After traversing the entire loop, she made her way back to her scooter to retrieve her things. If ever she wanted to disconnect from the world, all she had to do was open a book. Once she got caught up in a good story, she was almost oblivious to anything around her. A good distraction would do the trick.

Just past the first curve of the trail, she came to a wooden bench with a high back. She dropped down on the seat, placed her book across her knees, and the bag of cookies at her side. The entire surface of the bench was marred with names etched into the grain. She traced her finger along the edges of a lopsided heart with initials carved into its center. Something in its simplicity made her smile. Love was such an easy thing for everyone else but her. Groaning inside, she opened the paper bag, lifted out a broken hunk of cookie, and took a nibble.

She had only made it to the first mention of Biddy Hart in the book's introduction when her attention was drawn to the sound of approaching footsteps. Buoyed by an unexpected anticipation, she waited several seconds before lowering the book to her lap. Without making it look obvious, she eased back on her eagerness, washing away all signs that she might be happy to see him. As cool as could be, she turned her head, gazing through her heavy lashes. In a flash, she dropped her focus to the waiting book, biting back her disappointment on seeing the young couple strolling hand and hand. She kept her gaze fixed on the page's black print until they passed. As she watched the two lovers continue down the path, she dipped into the bag and brought another cookie to her lips. It was the couple's closeness that held her interest. The whole world could go up in a blaze and they would not have noticed, being far too absorbed in each other.

Over the years, there was never a shortage of guys vying for her attention. Being a free spirit, she was the exact opposite of what any good mother would want for her son. Attracting men was never the problem—guys sought her out when they were going through their rebellious stage—but getting rid of them could be an issue. Something about her made men fall head over heels. The more non-committal she acted, the more they clung to her. She had never once surrendered her heart, or let herself love someone back. In the end, every relationship ended with the same amount of desolation as a tornado across the great plains. The only thing she had ever been good at was leaving broken pieces.

Now, in the quiet of the woods, watching love bloom, she wondered what it would be like if she tried just once to be different. This had to be her lowest point, and something in her brought up the urge to call Adelia. It had been so long since they'd spoken, and she wasn't even sure her friend knew she was in Ireland. As much as she wanted to reach out, there was no way she could do so without feeling shame.

In truth, she was jealous. Growing up, it had always been she who advised Adelia on every predicament. Presenting herself as a straight shooter, she told her what she should say and do. She approached everything with a 'buck up, buttercup' attitude, forcing Adelia out of her comfort zone to face her fears head on. But it had all been a manufactured lie, to ease the girl's worry and make herself appear to be the worldly one. Her wisdom was as fake as her mother's hair color. Clairol, platinum blonde.

Deep down, she no longer had a shred of love for herself. Adelia had gone on to achieve great things already, moving to England, falling in love, and finishing college in high esteem. By contrast, she had all but failed at every single venture. Now that she had alienated everyone in her life, she needed a friend more than ever. Perhaps, for once, she could be the one seeking advice. Was it time to accept that she had brought herself to this bleak place and needed help getting out? Later, when she got back to the inn, she would make that call.

She cracked open her book once more, but barely read another paragraph before she closed it again. Her date with herself was turning out to be an utter flop. She unsnapped her satchel and fumbled around for her notebook, then browsed over the list of places she had noted.

"Dromore Woods," she said aloud. It was probably half an hour away but sounded worthwhile. She trailed her finger down the page. "Hmm... Woodlands, meadows, lake, river, and a castle. Castle? Yes, please."

She stuffed another cookie in her mouth, clenching it between her teeth as she gathered up her belongings. It was still early afternoon, giving her plenty of time to make the trip to Dromore and be home before nightfall. In reality, it didn't matter when she got back to Doonagore House. It wasn't as if anyone would be waiting for her.

****

Kate pulled off the road onto an overgrown stretch of what looked to have once been a gravel path for logging trucks. Back in time, Dromore Woods had been the seat of the O'Brien clan. The ruins of the castle, built by Teige O'Brien, stood at the edge of Dromore Lough just outside of Ruan on the northside of the woodland. The lands had passed down through several prominent families before being acquired by the Irish State in the 1940's. Mostly used as a commercial woodland now, but still frequented by locals as a favorite recreational spot.

She parked her scooter behind some tall grass, threw her satchel over her shoulder, and headed out to explore. As she walked along, having no idea where she was headed, she took note of anything that might serve as a visual marker for her return. The tall grass of the old road scratched at her bare legs, and tiny burs clung to the hemline of her dress. Just as she was about to turn back and seek out a better route into the woods, she caught sight of a narrow, well-kept trail that led from the edge of the road into the thick canopy of lush green trees. She paused to pluck the spiny little buggers off her dress and brushed her hands over her itchy skin, cursing herself for even bothering to pull this damn thing out of the closet. It hadn't made an appearance since she came to Ireland. She let out an irritated growl at herself, well aware of the reason she'd opted for this unsuitable attire—a plan that hadn't panned out.

The path led her into an area that looked like something straight out of the J.R.R. Tolkien books she'd grown to love. As she walked, each breath held faint wisps of earth, decaying wood, and wild garlic. A rich layer of moss carpeted the forest floor, and gnarled trees covered in creeping ivy towered over her, looming like giants waiting to reach out and grab her at any moment. Emerald-green ferns fanned out along the sides of the pathway, with tiny purple flowers peeking up through heavy layers of foliage. Puffs of wild mushrooms climbed the bark of fallen trees, reminding her of the colorful array of candy in the old general store down the block from her home back in Boston. As she moved along, wood mice scampered through the undergrowth, and red squirrels darted about the branches as they hopped from tree to tree. She felt like Alice in Wonderland, waiting for her own white rabbit to whisk her away on some wild adventure.

Deeper into the verdant forest she traveled, soaking in the natural tapestry, but the white rabbit never came. The solemn energy of her isolation was only curbed by the indescribable beauty of her surroundings. By now, she was feeling tired but kept going, almost afraid of what she would miss if she turned back. The place was too magical to stop, its essence filling her soul, almost as if she had been called to it.

As she rounded a bend in the trail, rays of sunlight burst through the leaf-rich awning. She scanned ahead, tracking the golden shimmer through the border of thick shade to the ground, and stopped dead in her tracks. There, just off in the distance, perched on an old hollowed-out tree trunk, was... not the white rabbit she had been anticipating, but none other than Old Gus's fair-haired hero. She was anything but disappointed.

He smiled at her, the golden hue of his lashes almost reflecting the sun. The man looked like a pot of gold at the end of a rainbow. Kate realized her mouth was open, and snapped it shut. It was impossible that Finn could have known she would arrive here at Dromore Woods. It was impossible. Wasn't it?

The remote isolation of her journey had been relaxing, but there was also a touch of eeriness in being out here alone. She took a few slow steps forward, trying to convey the sense that the sight of him wasn't filling her with a delightful zing from head to toe.

"I'm on a date, you know?" he said, mimicking her.

She stopped again, struggling to capture the right words. It wasn't long before Finn's devilish smile brought out her natural need to engage with a willing adversary.

"Is it going well?" she asked. "I hope he is a nice guy."

"Actually, don't say anything but I am starting to find him a little dull."

"Aah, I think I know that guy. He is one of those who knows it all, and a terrible listener, if you ask me."

"I didn't ask you, but thanks just the same." He laughed, jumped to his feet, stepped forward, but then stopped. "How is your date going?"

She tilted her head to the side, regarding him for a moment. He was so good looking. The sweetest kind of torture for a woman prone to jumping off the ledge without so much as bothering to consider where she might land.

"Not as well as I had hoped," she said, turning her head to look at nothing, just to keep from staring at him like a smitten fool. "We don't seem to have much in common. I was actually thinking about making up some excuse to duck out early."

He took a cautious step forward, as if he wasn't sure she would be a willing partner in this little dance.

"Aye, let me guess—she is one of those overly opinionated types. As warm and cuddly as a Tyrannosaurus Rex. Always going on about how she has everything under control. She can do it—"

"Yes! Yes!" she interrupted with a ferocious snap, taking another step in his direction. "I think we all get the picture," she added, not concerning herself that by "we all," she meant the two of them.

Her breath caught when he stepped forward, bridging the gap between them. She dropped her gaze, aware of the sudden burst of heat slithering through her cheeks and gathering behind her ears. It was as if she couldn't quite understand how to act in his presence.

Gathering her courage, she looked up to see that he had stopped a couple of feet from her, his closeness nearly knocking her off her center of gravity. The mere scent of him was enough to dissipate her reservations. She bit her lip as he stretched out an open hand.

"What do you say we leave these two to their own devices and go find that castle you've been wanting to see?"

She was about to take his hand but stopped herself. "How...? How did you know I wanted to see the castle?" She stared at him in disbelief, as if she might wake at any moment to find she was Alice and had dozed off on a blanket of mossy earth.

"You're a girl, Kate. All girls want to see a castle. Why else would you go traipsing around a muddy wood in a dress? Which looks lovely by the way."

"Really?" She smoothed the blue fabric across the curve of her hips. While she hadn't been fishing for a compliment, she would take it just the same. She was gripped by an urge to give a twirl, like a little girl in a frilly new Easter dress. Oh, who was she kidding? That was why she had worn the stupid thing.

Embarrassed by her burst of vanity, she steeled herself. "I will have you know I came to see the castle because I take a keen interest in Irish history. Not because I am... a girl."

"But you do like castles, right? You have always liked castles. You loved all those whimsical fairytales you read as a child, about dashing young princes who rescued willful maidens from the clutches of dragons and evil villains."

She glared so hard at him, she squinted. "Everybody likes those stories. That doesn't prove anything. I suppose you think of yourself as one of those princes who saves the princess in the high tower. Probably want me to pretend I am some damsel in distress to feed your frail ego."

Not that she would ever dare tell him, but she always loved those stories as a child, though she never thought herself pretty enough to be the princess. She wasn't a thin rail he could heave over his shoulder and dash off to safety. No, she always thought herself more qualified for the starring role as the dragon. The truth was that, all these years later, she had wandered far from that dreamy-eyed child. That sense of magic had been replaced by a new version of Kate McCarthy, jaded and ever skeptical, always reminding herself that those old stories had no place in her life.

"I have never been one to want a damsel in distress," he said. "I rather find myself drawn to the ones that cause distress. I like the way it feels to have to work for something."

Being July, it was already warm, but the temperature jumped at least ten degrees for Kate. Tiny beads of perspiration prickled her brow, though she dared not draw attention by trying to wipe them away. It was of little use, because Finn's gaze was fixed on every feature. In the light streaming through the trees, he studied her with the same intensity she did him. Neither seemed disappointed with what they saw.

He tilted his head. "Why are you blushing?"

The temperature jumped again for her. She wasn't sure if she was more embarrassed by the question or that a man such as him had a genuine interest. However, he'd put her on the spot, which she loathed. She was the queen of distraction tactics, expert at maneuvering her way out of any type of pressure. Not with Finn, though. Since the day she'd met him, she had not fared so well in that endeavor.

"I'm not blushing. It's just warm." She looked around. "It is really warm."

He produced a halfcocked grin, then raised his still-outstretched hand. "Shall we, oh damsel of distress?"

Self-conscious about the dampness of her palm, she hesitated for a second before releasing a melodramatic sigh. For reasons she couldn't explain, she had the sudden need to let go of every reason why she should say no. Just this once, it might be nice to feel that sense of magic she had lost long ago.

Relenting, she slid her hand into his, the feel of those long fingers intertwining with hers downright exquisite. The young couple back at the glen flicked into her mind. She had been in relationships before, and the act of holding someone's hand was not foreign to her. Never in any of those, though, had she experienced such unguarded closeness. Such a novel feeling, and she couldn't process it right away.

For once, she didn't dwell on the need to understand her feelings, so let them come as they may. Living in the moment brought a certain sense of euphoria—a high that came with taking a risk and not caring about the outcome. It was a walk in the woods, for goodness sakes, nothing to over-analyze. She let the sense of adventure take hold, seeing herself as the princess in the tower, squinting at the bright light when the bolted door swung open after years of being held captive. The heat of Finn's body surged through her bare arm, and she had the notion that today might well be the day the fairytale gets a whole new twist.

Chapter Eight

From the edge of the forest, a trail led toward the lake, through a meadow of tall grass. The well-worn path headed out onto a small peninsula where the roofline of O'Brien Castle jutted into the sunshine. It was no more than a fragment of what would have once been a formidable structure and a defensive hold. A simple stone square tower stretched up four stories to the ruins of old battlements that lined the top, with a single chimney projecting to the skyline. Along the backside, a jagged remnant of one of the outer walls stood as testament to the fact that time had been anything but kind to this old building. It stood like a proud elderly woman reflecting on her life as she neared its end. Kate stood looking up at this still-regal structure, breathing its last days. It was battered and bruised, yet maintained too much dignity to succumb to its fate. The castle would fight until its last day, nursing its battle wounds like true badges of honor. Its strength radiated, almost infusing her veins. Like so many of the magical places in this land, an unshakable sense of connection could not be denied.

As they neared the romantic ruin, she noticed that all the windows and arrow slits had long since been filled in with mortar and stone. No sign remained of the gatehouse or any other buildings that once stood on the estate. The stones had likely been carted away and repurposed over the years. Even so, an ornately carved archway that once served as the entrance to the keep remained at the front. She glanced up to see a weathered placard carved into the stone.

"This castle was built by Teige, second sone of Conner."

She found it difficult to decipher the rest of the script, but had read up on this place a while back. All the lands of Dromore, along with the castle, had been granted to Teige's father, Conner, somewhere in the late-sixteenth century. The last of the O'Briens to own the estate left around 1689, whereafter the castle fell into disrepair. Later attempts were made to restore it but the cost and time needed proved too much for those ambitious enough to try. Left to the elements, nature did what nature does, reclaiming what is rightfully hers.

Though little remained, it still hadn't lost its splendor. Just standing in its shadow had Kate feeling like a dreamy-eyed child. She let go of Finn's hand and walked out a few paces to take in the view. The ruin was situated on a narrow stretch of land bordered by thick ancient forest and the lake. Its setting was like a picture in a gallery, with all the details in vibrant color. She tried to imagine what it might have been like waking up each day to what looked like something out of a dream. It was so beautiful, she wanted to absorb it all at once, soak it up so the feeling remained, because this was a place that filled you with sorrow on leaving. It was a pity she hadn't brought her art supplies. This would have been a magnificent place to sketch.

"You like it here," Finn said, a smile in his eyes as he watched her all but become a blubbering fool over the beauty before her.

"I hadn't thought it would be quite this lovely," she replied. "I know Ireland is littered with ruins like these, but it is not the case where I am from. We have old buildings and beautiful places, don't get me wrong, but not like this, or nowhere near as old."

She stepped over to the corner of the tower and ran her hands along the stone's rough surface. It was like she could almost feel the echoes of the history that had passed within these walls.

"Just to be able to touch something this old takes my breath away."

She'd been grappling with this since the day she landed on these emerald shores. Having always had an appreciation for history, she held a special regard for literature and art. Yet there was something in Ireland's history that felt so special. It was a place where the human element felt particularly strong. This land had endured centuries of hardships, but no ordeal ever seemed to lessen the resilience of the people. Every ancient landmark held just as much pride as it did woe, each imprinted with the unbreakable spirit of generations of grit and toil.

"Shall we go inside?" Finn asked, as if it were something everyone did on an everyday run-of-the-mill Tuesday.

"We can't go inside," she said. "It isn't open to visitors. Besides, that gate has a fairly good-sized padlock." She pointed to the large metal device that hung heavy and imposing off the gate.

Finn shot her a self-assured grin. He stood back a few feet as he scanned the barrier.

"It's not iron," he said with a nod, stepping forward. "That wooden door behind the gate is too new to be original to the place."

He lifted the weighty monstrosity of a lock in both hands, as if judging whether it would be a worthy opponent. At one semi-firm tug, the lock opened, with all the resistance of a piece of tissue paper. His eyes twinkled in satisfaction.

Kate cracked a bemused smile at him. Though she didn't bother to point it out, she was convinced the hunk of metal must have been faulty and she had not witnessed some display of superhuman strength. No need to spoil his moment of triumph.

"Shall we?" he said, having unfastened the lock from the gate. He held it out to her, as if offering it as a cheap gift shop souvenir.

She cupped her hand beneath his.

"We can't go in there, Finn. We could get into a great amount of trouble. You should put that back right now."

Growing up, she had been a regular thorn in her parents' side, but always stopped short at breaking the law. When a few classmates in her high school science class made plans to meet up one night at an abandoned subway station, she faked a toothache to get out of it. She caused her parents enough stress being obstinate and indecisive, she wasn't about to add vandalism and breaking and entering to the list.

O'Brien Castle had been locked for a reason. Waltzing into a building not intended for visitors felt like a way to wreck what had so far been a fairly good afternoon. She didn't bother to try to hide her apprehension, sure it was scrawled across her face.

"This is history, Kate. Time belongs to no man. This is your castle. The one you have dreamed about since you were a little girl. You are going to get your castle today. I just don't think I can make good on the whole dragon thing."

With a nonchalant toss, he flung the lock to the ground. It landed with a dull thud. She had no idea why she trusted him as much as she did, other than he hadn't given her much reason not to. Something in her heart warmed at how much it meant to him that she should see this castle, or at least its remnants. She couldn't recall anyone ever going to such lengths to give her something like this. Even though she'd tried to play it off, Finn knew how much she wanted to explore this old-time capsule. He wanted this for her, and that made it all the more enticing.

Her logical side, the one she rarely allowed to get a word in edgewise, could hear her cautious mother scolding her for such folly, beside herself knowing her daughter was out here with a man she hardly knew, trespassing in a boarded-up castle, no less. Of all the perplexing emotions Finn evoked in her, she never felt unsafe in his presence. Quite the opposite. If there was any risk at all, it was in succumbing to his charms. While his charms were no doubt plentiful, she knew herself to be quite capable of resisting any man.

She could shake him off anytime she chose. At the moment, she had no desire to do so.

Throwing caution to the wind, she pulled her satchel over her head and set it against the wall. With a nervous smile, she reached out, letting her fingers twine with his. He smiled at that and, for a wordless moment, something almost surreal passed between them.

With his free hand, he pulled open the arched gate, resting his back against it to keep it propped. He guided her forward, positioning her in front of him before leaning in close. The rise and fall of his chest was warm against her back, and she shivered at the tickle of his breath along the side of her neck. Next, he looped his arms under hers, placed the flats of his palms on the wooden door, and gave a gentle push. The wood released an unearthly groan, and Kate lowered her eyelids, expecting a musty cloud of dust to come rushing at them but, instead, the space lit up with a flash of light, and she was far too curious not to look up. And what a sight. The dark recesses of the stone corridor ahead glowed with a heavy fog almost lavender in color, with shimmering gold flakes that twisted and turned with an iridescent glimmer. The air was perfumed with something sweet that filled her head with images of fresh-cut spring blooms.

In disbelief, she turned to Finn, forgetting how close he was, and brushed her lips against his jaw. She pulled away, but he didn't budge, standing still as if lost in his own moment. Then his hand came to rest on the small of her back and he gave her a gentle nudge. She stepped forward, her toes meeting with the uneven cobbles.

The luminous mist lit up the entryway to reveal a curved stone staircase to the right and another arched doorway to the left. Up ahead looked to be the remainder of the hallway that probably once led further into the castle, but had since been blocked off.

"Welcome home, Princess," Finn said.

She pulled away to face him, then gave his shoulder a playful push. "I suppose you are the prince, then?"

"Sadly, I am the only prince left," he answered, his smile dripping with mirth. "I fed all the others to the dragon."

"It appears my options have decreased substantially." She stepped back to look him up and down, grinning. "I guess you will just have to do, for now."

It was Finn who first stepped through the doorway that led to one of the side chambers. He grasped hold of her hand and led her into the large room, bordered by four gray stone walls. Centuries of abandonment had left the old slab floor crumbling, with loose fragments crunching beneath her feet. A big fireplace was set into the far wall, its mantle claimed by a substantial vine of invasive ivy that stretched up to holes where the wood-beamed ceiling once existed. Small blooms dotted the ivy, their deep amethyst hue softening the harshness of the empty room. In the corners, cobwebs hung like heavy drapes of English lace, and bright beams of sunlight poured down through the holes, illuminating the thin space between them.

Finn turned to look around the room. With his back to her, she wondered if he could feel the piercing heat of her stare. Here in the light of day, she was hungry to take in every exquisite detail of this man. She took advantage of this moment, when his attention was diverted long enough for her to soak him up. He radiated something that was almost magnetic, pulling her to him with such force that she could only find relief within his proximity. In his case, there was no such thing as too close. She could not recall ever feeling this way about anyone before.

She averted her gaze as he turned back to her. He executed a wide wave of his hand, like a master of ceremonies about to cue the curtain call.

"As lady of the house, you get to choose the decorating style. I warn you, though, no going out of budget like you did last time."

"I'm a princess, after all—I like the finer things. What can I say?" She shrugged, then pointed at the flourish of ivy climbing the wall. "I rather like this botanical style. Maybe some nice damask drapes and some lace doilies, and this place will feel just like home."

"Definitely the doilies," he said with a firm nod of agreement. "As the dashing prince, my subjects would want to know that I am surrounded with the very finest of doilies."

"Indeed, it is our duty to live as the people would expect."

"Just think of it," he said, placing his hands on his hips. "We could spend every night sitting here by the fire. You, reading your books of Irish fables, and me wowing you with tales of my chivalrous exploits."

"Do I have to be one of those airhead princesses who pretends everything you do is the most fantastic thing to have ever happened?"

"There will be no pretending. You will be awestruck by my every deed."

"I rather think I will need a very large collection of books," she said. "With all that incessant prattling, I will need something to occupy my time."

He raised his hand to his chin, the action slow, deliberate, his long fingers brushing his silky skin. "Such a well-read woman could be dangerous."

Kate pursed her lips, not impressed. "You are opposed to women who read?"

"On the contrary," he corrected. "A great prince requires a princess of equal valor, both in heart and mind. My darling, I shall fill a room with leather-bound tomes that touch the rafters for you. I require every last ounce of your wit in this kingdom. Nothing less will suffice."

Once again, heat inched along the curves of her throat, and she was sure he noticed the crimson flush. He stepped closer, until they stood toe to toe, and flashed a simple grin. His light was so bright, his warmth tangible. He pulled her to him, held one of her hands in the air, and wrapped his other around her waist. Every muscle in her body threatened to melt against his touch. With a smooth step to the side, he began to sway and turn until they were in a full waltz. Finn, to his credit, was a far more accomplished dancer than his partner, who did her best to keep time, though the prospect of rolling her injured ankle wasn't too far from her mind.

"Are all American girls so pretty?"

Pretty? Was he half blind? She would hardly consider herself competition for ninety-five percent of the girls she knew back home. In truth, she wasn't even confident enough to say her looks were mediocre, at best. Her jealous bone grew at the thought that he might come to realize this if he ever donned a decent pair of spectacles.

"No," she snipped, maybe a bit too fast. "There is no sun there, so they are all very pale. And most are gaunt from poor diet. Crooked backs and bulging eyes are fairly common."

He regarded her for the liar she was, but didn't bother to argue her ridiculous explanation, which amused her.

"There is another room for you to see, my lady. This way." He spun and swayed them toward a small doorway in the back wall. As they entered a short hallway, Kate squinted against a flood of daylight. At the end of the passageway, a single stone step dropped into what was once an enormous room of some kind. Unlike the rest of the four-storied keep, this space had nothing above it but open air. The entire back wall was gone, replaced by a border of thick foliage and mature trees. It was hard to discern just what it would have been back in the glory days. In one swift motion, Finn lifted her down the step and planted her with a smile on the floor. The rush of air flared out the bottom of her dress, making her feel as dainty as a ballerina.

He took her back into his arms and resumed his slow sway. She blinked several times, her head to the side, ears strained. For a fleeting moment, she could have sworn there was music.

"What is this room," she asked her dance partner.

"I don't know," he answered. "It might take some remodeling, but let's just make this the open-air kitchen. Each and every night we will dance in here as the sun sets."

"I feel like that would be annoying to the cooks, having us always in their way."

"Wait? You're not going to cook my dinner every night?"

"I should say not. I am a princess, you know. Besides, I am actually a terrible cook. I have had several near misses in the past. Let's just say, if I am in the kitchen, you are likely to see members of your local fire department that day."

"Ooh, best we stick with the cooks, then. We'll just build a nice big kitchen, with plenty of room for dancing."

"A dancefloor in the kitchen? Sounds completely logical."

After a spin or two through the future kitchen dance hall, Finn took her once again by the hand and led her back along the narrow hallway, across the first room, and toward the stone staircase, its spiral steps winding up to the next floor. They were uneven in height, with each one worn in the center from years of use. His grip tightened on her hand as she took them one by one, using her free hand to brace herself against the wall. At the first landing, he stood to the side, and she peered through the doorway onto the battered remnants of the floor. The ivy from below continued its way up the wall to what little remained of the vaulted roof, and the two stories above revealed the tell-tale markings of the inserts that had once held the floor beams. Leaning out to get a closer look, she felt Finn fumble as he grasped hold of her waist.

"Don't lean out too far. I don't trust that old floor."

"Me neither," she said, shuffling back a few inches and resting against his chest. "What will this room be? After a few repairs, of course."

"Well, this will be the nursery. I'd say it looks to be large enough to hold at least seventeen young strapping boys."

"Oh... seventeen? Children? That is a bit too tall of an order. Can we change it to cats, by chance?"

"A nursery with seventeen cats." He mulled it over for a moment. "Splendid idea, Princess. Perhaps we should consider hiring an extra servant or two to keep up on the shedding."

"I think that is best. As a princess, I won't have time for all that manual labor."

"Plus, you will be wholly devoted to your prince." He arched a hopeful brow.

"I feel like the cats will need a lot of attention, and I will have to fill my time with their care. You are a grown man, you can darn your own socks, love."

He wrinkled his nose at her. The cats were going to be a source of contention in this fairytale.

They continued climbing the steps, assigning each level its role in their growing story. At the last curve in the staircase, before the opening that led out to the rooftop, her mind flickered back to a print that hung on her bedroom wall back in Boston. 'The Meeting on the Turret,' by Frederic William Burton, depicted the last moments between Hellelil and Hildebrand before Hildebrand faced death. It had always been her favorite—equal parts tenderness and tragedy.

As Finn helped her through the small opening to the battlement, she blinked against the brightness of the sun. She took great care stepping out, the thin air bringing renewed reality as she looked down at the ground so far below. They were way higher than she had imagined. Maybe Finn's endless waltzing had caught up because she still felt her body spinning, even though she knew she was frozen in place. She gripped his arm, her fingertips almost digging into his flesh. In this moment, the memory of the painting resonated with her more than ever, as if its meaning had become the ballad of her life.

"What's the matter?"

The shift of concern in his voice was clear.

"I don't do so well with heights. Just give me a second and I will be fine." Her breath came in rapid puffs, matching her thundering heartbeat.

With Finn gripping her waist, steadying her in place, she took a long deep breath, eyes clenched tight, holding onto his forearms as though she were clutching a life preserver in a stormy sea.

"After a long hard day of princing—"

"Darling," she choked out, looking back at him, "I must interrupt you. I am quite sure that *princing* is not actually a word. Might we go with... *being princely*?"

He frowned, then pursed his lips before his features softened. "As the prince, couldn't I just make it a word?"

She smiled, appreciating his attempt at distracting her. It had worked, but she couldn't let him away with everything. "I'd firmly advise against that kind of leadership. Your subjects might be greatly opposed to you trifling with the English language. It could end up leading to a full-scale rebellion. All that political back and forth." She heaved out a long sigh. "In the end, I think it would be better for our relationship if you just didn't create new words."

He squeezed his chin, tapping his forefinger against his cheek. "I certainly wouldn't want to jeopardize our relationship. After all, I slayed a dragon for you."

"No need to martyr yourself, darling. It was a small dragon."

"Boy, you are a tough one to impress. A touch bossy, too." He grinned.

"You call it bossy, I call it aggressively helpful." She allowed a soft smile. "I'm just trying to keep you grounded."

"With this kind of view to behold, Princess, I would say I am anything but grounded."

She looked out at the endless horizon. With the shimmer of the sun off the water, and the beauty of the thick forest, every inch of this place was carved out of a fairytale. When she turned back to Finn, she realized that his gaze had never left her. He didn't need to point it out because she knew that pink hue had returned to her cheeks.

"There is something else I want to show you," he said. He smiled at her expectant look, leaving her hanging in suspense.

In a flurry, she followed him down the stairs and out the front door of the castle. After fixing the padlock back on the gate, he turned to her.

"This is a place that is just for you, Princess. It's deep in the woods, and as far away from the angry world as you can ever get."

"Is it a secret place?"

"Just for you and I."

A place only they would know. Something in her awakened, something wild and undiscovered, that had her dizzy with anticipation. Whether it was the heat of his hand against hers, or that he had twirled her around in a fairytale castle, she couldn't be sure, but the feeling was far more dazzling than anything she had ever experienced.

He led her deep into Dromore woods. Veering off the main trail, they came upon a patch of large Hawthorn bushes that revealed a hidden path, its entrance further shielded by heavy ferns and long-fallen trees. The path, paved in thick green moss, dipped into a small gully before rising on the other side. Nervous, Kate glanced around, sure she would never be able to find her way back alone.

The pathway narrowed as it slinked between trees bordering both sides. Finn looked back with a smile and ducked his head beneath a natural trellis formed by intertwined limbs. As he moved forward, Kate caught sight of a vine of large ripe berries. The cookies from earlier were a distant memory, so she plucked a few off and popped them into her mouth. The burst of flavor was exquisite, and she snagged a few more, clutching them in her palm before scurrying to catch up with Finn who was already coming out at the other end.

As she stepped out from under the last limb, she could hardly believe her eyes. Finn stood in the center of a circle formed by a low dry-stone wall, its floor of thick green grass almost covered by tiny yellow blooms, making it look like a blanket of gold.

She knelt to touch one of the flowers. "They're buttercups. Thousands and thousands of buttercups." Her breath caught, and she held her hand to her chest. "I have never seen anything like it."

Finn flashed a dazzling smile, his pride in his surprise clear. Kate stepped closer, still full of wonder at the golden glow of the tiny blooms. She stretched her arms out and spun around, letting out a laugh of pure amazement.

"I have never seen anything this pretty."

"Me neither," he said, continuing to watch her.

She unfastened her satchel at her side and pulled out her rolled-up blanket.

"Are you cold?" he asked. "It is the warmest day we have had all summer."

"No, silly, I am actually a bit tired. I'm pretty sure we have covered a few miles today, and I think I am due to sit down for a bit."

As she tried to open the blanket, it became apparent that it wasn't going to be easy with the berries in her other hand. She tucked the blanket under her arm and popped two berries into her mouth.

"What is that?" he asked, his tone demanding more than curious.

"Oh, these? I got them off the vine back there."

"At the entrance?" He stepped closer, scrutinizing the last remaining berry, now half-squished.

Her tummy flipped, and she chucked it on the grass. "They aren't poisonous, are they?"

He cupped his chin for a long moment, as if deep in thought. His Adam's apple bobbed as he swallowed. "No, they aren't poisonous. Best not to eat anything around here, though."

It was against her natural inclination but she didn't bother to ask why. Maybe she was too tired. She fanned out the blanket across a patch of buttercups, flopped down on it, straightened the bottom of her dress, and stretched out her legs. Then she reached down and rubbed at her injured ankle. For as much trouble as it had been before, she hadn't felt a shred of pain during their adventure, including all the waltzing. Even if it didn't make much sense, she wasn't about to complain.

Finn took his place beside her, rolling onto his back and folding his hands behind his head. Her eyelids grew heavy, and she wondered if it had anything to do with the berries, or was it just the full day catching up? When she glanced down at her empty wrist, she remembered her watch that was still lying on her bedside table at home. She looked up at the sky, trying to discern how late it was, to no avail, but she didn't care, she would get home eventually. With a contented sigh, she slid down to lie on her back, closed her eyes, and let the warmth of the sun take over.

"Finn?"

"Yes, Princess."

"Don't you wish everyday could be like today?"

"It can be," he replied. "Just say the word."

She had no idea what she needed to say to have all her troubles washed away, to live her life tucked deep in the woods in a secret field of buttercups. It mattered little because, before she could speak, the warmth of his lips covered hers, and all the world, both real and imaginary, faded away.

Chapter Nine

Kate's eyes fluttered open as Finn's lips lifted from hers. Never had she experienced such a gorgeous kiss, its residual energy tingling in her toes. It took a moment for her eyes to adjust, and then the confusion set in. They were standing at her door back at Doonagore House. It was late, the sun had already set, and her brain was foggy with questions. How could they be here? How did they get back?

"My... s-scooter?" she stammered. It was a somewhat random concern given the present situation, but she still wanted to know.

"It is parked in its usual spot," Finn said. He pulled the strap of her satchel from his shoulder and handed it over.

She blinked several times as she stared at his hand, her senses delayed. Without a word, she took the bag and set it at her feet.

Finn pulled her hand into his and placed a quick peck on her knuckles. "Until we write the next chapter of our fairytale." And with that, he stepped away, fading back into the night.

She stood there for a few minutes, taking in the quietness, reviewing her day. The disorientation of how she had turned up at her doorstep aside, she realized she was at a dangerous impasse. Today proved she felt something for Finn, and it was apparent that he felt something in return, but whatever existed between them was different to anything she had known before. This was the only time she could recall having no control over her heart. Guarding her emotions was almost a well-honed skill—probably the only real talent she possessed—but with Finn, her defenses were weakening. Perhaps she had overestimated her ability to resist him, because there was no denying she was vulnerable to his charm, being one dashing smile, or long gray-eyed gaze away from becoming the thing she despised most, a mushy lovesick fool.

At this point there were only two things she knew for certain: First, berries in a secret meadow tucked deep in an ancient forest were a bad idea for a late-day snack. Second, she had to rely on her brain to keep its good senses, because her heart was proving to be the worst kind of traitor.

A few days later, as Kate was headed to start a dayshift at reception, her uncle Liam met her on the way. She could tell he had something pressing on his mind. Liam was the type who was no good at disguising his thoughts, his face betraying him every time. He began the conversation with a few pleasantries, asking about her day, remarking on the weather. Just like him, she was as poor at camouflaging her inner dialog. From all accounts, her green eyes became as analyzing as a detective in an interrogation room. It wasn't long before Liam cut to the chase.

"Your... dad phoned me today," he said with a nervous pause.

Kate realized he was trying to read her reaction, so remained neutral.

"I know that things between you and your folks weren't exactly great when you left, but they really want to see you."

"I am sure they do," she said, her defiance seeping through.

"You are their only child, Kate. They want to make it right between you."

The pleading in his eyes made her soften. Her anger had nothing to do with him, and it wasn't fair to put him in the middle any more than the poor man already was. Until now, she had never considered the trouble he and Edel suffered by taking her on.

"I'm just not ready to talk to them yet," she said, keeping her voice soft.

"Well... that makes it difficult because they are coming in two weeks' time." He grimaced. "You have to do this some day. Might as well make it sooner than later. It is going to take some giving on both sides."

"I'm not ready to leave," she said, acknowledging to herself that it was a personal confession. "I like it here."

"You don't have to leave," he assured. "Hell, I would keep you here for good if it was my choice. You are by far the only one I know who can keep Seán in his place. Just talk to your parents, is all I ask.

You have time to think it through, but, ultimately, only you know what has to be done."

She didn't respond, not wanting to make false promises when he and Edel had done so much for her. This wasn't a matter she could consider in a short time. She needed to think it through.

"What do you say you let me cover the front desk this morning? I could really use you in the pub tonight, anyway."

She could hardly argue. The prospect of crawling back into bed and wallowing in her own self- misery sounded delightful. She needed time to overthink her overthinking.

That evening, when she reported to the pub for her shift, she found she would be working there for the next few weeks. In truth, it was the job she preferred above all others. Working at the front desk made for a painfully slow day. Not to mention it was usually an early shift, and her penchant for sleepless nights made it all the more difficult.

The pub was a far livelier place. A few nights a week, local musicians would come in for traditional Irish sessions. Doolin was the local hub for all things music, with no shortage of talent in the wider area. She loved that people left all their troubles at the door. For that brief amount of time, it made her forget she had problems of her own.

That night's music had just begun when Old Gus entered through the front door. Though he always stayed humble, he had become something of a celebrity in these parts. He gave a friendly wave to a few of the patrons and eased his way toward Kate as she wiped down the counter.

"You have seen your suitor again," he declared, loud enough for all of the neighboring tables to hear.

Her face flushed with a deep heat, and she was sure the resultant crimson made the vibrant shade of her hair dull in comparison.

"What gave you that impression?" she asked through gritted teeth.

"Love puts a light in your eyes and makes you feel like you're walking on your tiptoes. It is just like a pond frog." He smiled to himself. She gave him a blank stare, the same one he'd been on the receiving end of many times. "Easy to catch, but hard to hold onto," he added, unphased by her confusion.

She stared harder. "That's an interesting analogy."

"He is a nice fellow? Well-mannered?"

"He is a real gentleman." Though she managed a straight face, she knew Old Gus had caught the sparkle in her eyes.

"A gentleman, aye. Sometimes it's difficult to discern a gentleman and a villain. They can look quite similar." He looked as if he was anticipating her usual sharp-tongued response.

"Soft day out there," she said, sidestepping his expectations like a céilí dancer.

"It will be bucketing down later, mark my words," he replied, shaking his finger at her, as if swearing a sacred oath.

She didn't miss the twinkle in his eye as he pulled his hat from his head and set it on the bar counter. With anyone else in these parts, a word on the weather was a sure-fire way to derail the entire conversation. But Old Gus was far too sharp for the likes of her blatant attempt at manipulation, and she expected more from him later on.

"I will get your tea ready," she said, and reached over to pull his usual cup from the shelf.

After pouring his tea, she turned to grab his brown sugar when Seán's deep bellow resounded above the music. The man was never content to make a quiet entrance, enjoying the attention, good or bad, he received from making his presence known. She thought back to her short stint in college. Her psychology professor would have delighted in making an in-depth study of someone like Seán. She imagined he would explain some low-lying insecurity tucked away deep in his subconscious, and how it could only be satisfied by the knowledge that his presence was known to every person in the room.

She watched his approach. He flopped down on the stool next to Old Gus, slapping his hands on the counter, so hard he nearly threw the musicians off beat. She pursed her lips, her psychological assessment validated. Yes, her old professor would have said she'd hit the nail right on the head.

"What's the craic there, Gus?" He waved a finger at Kate, signaling his usual order.

She glared at him for trying to herd her around like a prize heifer. However, being that he was still a paying customer, she had little choice but to comply with his request, though she did so drenched in quiet defiance.

"Oh, I was just asking Miss McCarthy about her suitor."

"He is not my suitor," she snapped, Seán's glass nearly overflowing with her distraction. Though, after the other day, she was softening to the idea.

"Oh, I would stick to your Finnley, Miss McCarthy. I just heard that the old postman's health has taken a turn for the worse. He may well be off the market soon. Only date you will get out of him is at the wake." He chuckled to himself, oblivious to her grimace at his morbid humor. She found it an off-putting comment, even for Seán. Then again, if her time in County Clare had taught her anything, it was that the Irish had a soft spot for dark humor. Much like his comment about her looking like Maureen O'Hara once had, she granted him yet another free pass.

"Soft day, isn't it?" she responded, garnering a mischievous grin from Gus.

"Soft day?" Seán fired back. "You wouldn't put the dog out in it. It's sideways rain, and, Jayses, that wind could cut ya."

She looked past him to the front window. It was a dirty-looking sky, but the rain had all but stopped. No need to correct him on that point when he was already onto another topic.

Just as she was about to step out to clean off one of the tables, Liam came in through the back, looking flustered.

"Do you need something?" she inquired as he fumbled through the cash register.

"It has been a busy day, and I forgot to go and pay Mrs. Brennan for the curtains she hemmed for me last week. I need to get this out to her this evening, but I have a tap in one of the guest rooms that needs fixing."

Kate knew he was referring to a faucet, but felt no need to say it. He ran his fingers through his short brown hair, then tugged on the strands as if he might pull them out.

"You'll have to give me directions, but I could run it out to her," she offered, afraid the poor man would do damage to his scalp. He was always keen on doing things himself, so she doubted he would agree, but she felt obliged to make the suggestion.

"Well..." He pulled his lips into a thin line, his expression pained. "I could have one of the other girls fill in for you. It's not that far. Wouldn't take you long, but I feel inclined to warn you Mrs. Brennan is a talker. She will bend your ear a good while if you let her."

"How far is it?" By now the pub was in full swing, and a break from the noise, and Seán, sounded good.

"A little way out. Maybe a mile past Cahermann."

She almost came to attention. Finn had said he lived on Cahermann Hill. Was Mrs. Brennan's house close by? Maybe she knew him. She caught herself on, assuring herself that she did not care in the least. Right now, she needed to slow down. She was losing her wits over him.

Liam took a pencil and paper from a nearby drawer and drew out a crude map, then folded several cash notes and placed them into a small envelope, which he handed to her. As he disappeared back through the doorway, heading to find her replacement, Old Gus remained silent. Kate took off her apron, aware that he was watching her.

"You make a point to head out there to Mrs. Brennan's and get yourself right back before nightfall."

She stared at him, feeling like she was being lectured by her grandfather. Besides, she knew it couldn't take all that long. For her, the speed limit was simply a suggestion, one she routinely ignored.

"Biddy Early would tell you to be past Spectacle Bridge before the sun sets. Nothing good could come of it if you are not."

"Biddy Early?" Kate repeated, confused. The name didn't ring a bell, but that didn't come as a surprise. She still didn't know a good many people in the area. Yet, something about the woman's name filled her with an odd sense of trepidation.

"Biddy was a bean feasa—a wise woman. A seer of sorts. She lived out in Feakle, east of here. While Biddy died a great many years ago, there was nothing that woman said then that doesn't hold true now. If she told you something, you would do well to follow it to the letter. Be it the Good People or something far darker, it doesn't matter—nothing good awaits you if you cross over that bridge after nightfall. Hurry home now."

Something resembling terror flooded her gut. A seriousness in Old Gus's eyes told her this was not a simple recommendation. And while she wasn't one to believe in most of the tales he told, this time felt different. She shuddered, aware of a strange pull, as if she were being led toward something, or perhaps away.

Even Seán's face had a stony expression. He swallowed hard, his Adam's apple bobbing. It unnerved her to see him like this, and so quiet. It wasn't that his silence was unpleasant – quite the opposite – but it was well out of his nature.

"It's almost eight o'clock," he said, tapping his finger on the counter. "Do as Old Gus says, and hurry back. I should think I will be long gone by the time you get back. The wife will have my head otherwise."

She glanced at her watch. The evening had flown by so fast. "Wait a minute, you are married?"

"More than thirty years." He gave a toothy grin, sliding his thumbs beneath the edge of his suspenders, like a farmer at the county fair whose pig had just won first prize.

"It just hit me. Here I am martyring myself for having to put up with you a couple hours a week in the pub, and some poor woman has to wake up to you every day? What has that unlucky creature done to deserve such cruelty?"

His wide smile faded into a hardened jaw. "Bet they threw a party the day you left Boston. Probably had a parade and free pints for every citizen."

Though she was sure he had no idea of the circumstances surrounding her departure from the States, his comment still hit close to home. As much as she'd come to love Ireland, a bitter sting lingered when she thought about what brought her here in the first place. Now that she'd been afforded ample time to reflect, there was no doubting her restless spirit had tested her parents' patience more than once. She couldn't blame them for wanting to escape the embarrassment. All she had ever done was defy their every wish. Her dose of karma, while deserved, still felt fresh. Now, with the prospect of seeing them again in two weeks, everything came flooding back to the surface.

"If you are gone when I get back, I just might buy the whole pub a round," she said, delighting in her parting shot as she walked toward the door.

Chapter Ten

Kate shuddered as her cranky Vespa crossed over Spectacle Bridge, leading out toward the road to Mrs. Brennan's. Try as she might to avoid it, there were times when Old Gus's fanciful tales stuck in her head. His stories, while entertaining, were just legends passed down by people who needed something to help explain away misfortunes and the occasional rare stroke of luck. No matter where you were, every place had its share of fables. Boston was rife with ghostly tales of spirits, and creatures that lurked in the back alleyways. Edgar Allan Poe was a Boston man himself. Kate had always pegged these as cautionary tales, and with the long dark hours of the night reserved for lovers and worried mothers, she could hardly fault any parent for not wanting to have their grown daughter out unsupervised. Yes, Old Gus was just serving the role of her mom and dad, who were so far away, for now.

Following Liam's directions, she made it through the breadth and length of the countryside out to her destination. The house was a simple single-story cottage, down a long gravel driveway. She parked near the front door and took out the envelope Liam had given her. There was such a stillness here—quiet and remote. She thought about Finn. His house couldn't be too far from this property. Why did his roaming nights lead him in search of a better place to find solitude, when this area had to be more than ideal to be alone with his thoughts? Maybe he preferred being closer to the coast.

She was surprised to see the tall thin woman who came to the door. Liam had called ahead, to alert her to an imminent visitor. Mrs. Brennan had come down with a cold and was cloaked in a heavy robe, her drawn face looking as though she was suffering the worst of her affliction. When Kate was offered a cup of tea, she thought it best to decline, insisting the woman head straight back to bed. As she walked to her scooter, she couldn't help but think she sounded like a stern parent to the older woman.

Back out onto the road, she glanced down at her watch. By now, she hoped Seán had departed, so she could resume her night in peace upon her return. Liam would be thrilled that she'd managed to break free from Mrs. Brennan so soon, though he wouldn't go so far as being thankful for the woman's ill health.

She had only traveled a mile or so when she felt a light knock in her scooter's engine. Then came a loud sputter as a pop of smoke billowed out the back. She let out a loud growl, but there was no one around to hear her. The road was desolate, save for a few grazing sheep and two or three cattle in the fields.

After several failed attempts to restart the engine, she pushed the scooter onto the soft grassy shoulder, nudged the kickstand into place, then stood back and surveyed the machine, as if she had a clue what was wrong or how to fix it. She wasn't mechanically inclined. In truth, she had never held a screwdriver. A low growl rumbled in her chest as she realized there wasn't even a house in sight. She unfastened her helmet and clipped it onto the bar on the back of the scooter where she strapped packages and bags when she went into the village.

With her anger bubbling up, she grabbed hold of the handlebars and gave the stand a vicious kick with her good foot. It lifted, and she yelped as the scooter lunged forward. The dead vehicle felt heavy, and she leveraged her body weight toward the front as she pushed it along the edge of the road, careful to stay as far over as possible should a motorist come thundering in her direction. By now, it was well past nine o'clock and the sun was starting its slow descent in the west. It was the middle of summer, and her only advantage was that she had at least a half-hour, maybe more before the sun fully set. At this snail's pace, chances were slim that she would make it back across the bridge before then. The best she could hope for was to find a house along the way, where they might let her ring Liam.

As she neared a bend in the road, something caught her attention—a rise in the landscape, surrounded by a low dry-stone wall. There upon the high part of the ridge stood a tall lean figure, the pinkish hue of the dusky sky folding around him like an ethereal glow. She didn't stop, trudging forward at an even gait, but she couldn't help but stare at the silhouette. Then the person moved, coming down the hill in her direction. She looked back to the road ahead, embarrassed at her plight. As the man came closer, she slowed her pace, then stopped. One by one, the details of his face came into view. It was him.

Her breath caught, and her lungs bucked against her for holding it too long. At the bottom of the hill, Finn dipped down through the side ditch and came back up, stopping just opposite her on the other side of the road.

"Were you looking for me?" he asked, his eyes gleaming.

The pit of her stomach fluttered. While she shouldn't have been happy to see him, given her current dilemma, she was just glad to no longer be alone out here. With this being her first time traveling this route, she had no real bearing of where she was, nor how long it would take to push this piece of junk back to the village.

"Why on earth should I be looking for you?" she snapped in jest. "I just like to walk out here sometimes."

"And push that?" He motioned to the useless pile of metal.

"The resistance is good for the heart. This is all part of my daily exercise routine."

He responded with a long unamused stare that bordered on the uncomfortable.

"I am willing to lend you my assistance, so long as you don't come at me like an angry badger for offering."

He gestured for her to let him take over, but she retained a firm grip on the handlebars. She didn't need his help, confident she was doing fine on her own, even if she was out of breath, panting like a sheepdog having just qualified in the trials.

"When have I ever come at you like an angry badger?" she asked, aware of its sharpness. In the exertion of pushing the scooter, she had managed to break a healthy sweat. Some of her red locks had broken loose from her ponytail, and hung like wet rags on a clothesline. She pushed them back from her face and tucked them behind her ear, as if the effort would make any difference.

"My memory is foggy, but I do recall having a bag of linens flung at me not so long ago. I think I still have a mark." He grimaced as he rubbed his abdomen over his shirt, and Kate caught herself staring far too long at the spot.

He was so pretty. Perfectly crafted, from the shimmer of his golden hair, the gentle lines of his face, and all the places beyond. Pretty was far from the best word to describe what she thought of his appearance, but it was all that came to mind as he stood there. Seeing him in the fading light of day sent a delightful sensation through her, like coming down the stairs on Christmas morning to see beautifully wrapped packages beneath the tree. He truly was something to behold.

It bothered her how he made her mind turn to absolute mush. He didn't have to do anything, just be close, and all the world seemed to disappear. The only other person who could do that to her was Elvis. That was it. Finn was her Irish Elvis, minus the hairstyle, guitar, and gyrations.

Something in the silence snapped her back to reality. Realizing that she was looking at him with an all but open-mouth drooling stare, she contemplated giving herself one of her trademark smacks across the face. She didn't, but she doubted Finn would have thought a thing of it if she had. At this stage, she'd already determined that he must think her the stupidest girl in the whole country.

"Give me the scooter," he said, in more of a demand than a request. "You won't be able to push it through the tall grass."

She glanced around. "Why would I push it through the grass?"

"We are going to my house," he stated, flicking a thumb in the direction he'd come.

"We are?"

He responded with a simple nod, as if there was no other option in the matter.

"We are," she agreed.

He took the handlebars and eased the dead beast across the road, down through the ditch and up the subtle incline. Kate trailed behind him, like a newborn puppy exploring its world for the first time, content to size him up as he glided ahead, and amazed at his ability to push her scooter through the thick grass with almost no effort.

On reaching the top of the rise, she stopped in her tracks. A large Georgian-style house stood square in the middle of the grassy field. It was two stories high, topped by a hipped slate roof, with two dormers jutting out in front. The corner quoins of pure white stone gave it a sophisticated look, echoing back to the crisp clean architecture of the time. While the house was beautiful, it felt out of place nestled in the simplicity of the landscape. No ornate gardens or stone walls surrounded it. It was almost as if someone had just thrown a stone and, wherever it landed, a house was built on that spot.

She released a delighted gasp, pretending to be oblivious to Finn's subtle grin as he watched her. When she glanced down the hill they had just ascended, she couldn't understand how it shielded such a large structure from the road. The hill wasn't high enough to shield a sheep from view.

"This is where you live?" she sputtered aloud.

"This is where I live," he said. He propped the scooter's kickstand into place, then beckoned her to follow. Still somewhat mesmerized, she complied.

As she crossed the distance to the front steps, a sense of familiarity reminded her of houses back in the States. Progress spelled the end for a great many buildings like this in Boston, but some managed to survive. Efficiency had not been a priority when houses such as this were built, and over time, many fell into disrepair. They were far too expensive for even the wealthiest of families to maintain, and quite a few were converted to museums or housed a multitude of offices. She thought back to her grade school days, touring one of the magnificent homes that had been restored to its former glory. A smile came unbidden as she tried to imagine what life would have been like living in something so beautiful.

Finn hopped up the front steps and stood at the door for a moment before opening it and inviting her in with a wide sweep of his arm. The entryway held a luxurious simplicity. Its walls were patterned with a matte-ivory damask print with shimmering emerald scrollwork intertwined. A polished hardwood floor led to the carved newel posts of a solid wood staircase that was lined with portraits of stoically faced subjects, all clad in the attire of generations past. Above, a low-hanging chandelier glowed, its brass arms holding delicately carved crystals that scattered fragments of light about the space like embers on the wind. The whole place felt suspended in time, as if its past inhabitants had just packed up and moved, leaving all possessions in their rightful spot. This time capsule, though beautiful, felt out of place in this era. It was more like a well-preserved tourist attraction than a home for a single man.

Had it been passed along through generations of Finn's family, rendering him with the responsibility of its preservation? The house, while beautiful, was far too small to rival some of the finer estates of bygone areas. At best, she guessed it had once served as a country home in its prime, perhaps even a wealthy landowner's hunting lodge. As she followed him through the halls, she couldn't help glance into the rooms she passed. A formal greeting room at the front led to what looked like something that had served as a den, complete with towering bookshelves that covered the greater part of the walls. A little further on, he walked into a great dining room, its long oak table set with fine china, as if a dinner party was about to commence.

"I really should ring Liam and let him know I had trouble on the way back," she called out, causing Finn to turn back to face her. "He will be worried if I don't return home before long."

"Liam?" His eyes flickered with what might have been a spark of jealousy, though she couldn't be sure.

"My uncle. He sent me out on an errand to Mrs. Brennan's house. I was supposed to come straight back, but obviously that plan was derailed. Can I use your phone to ring him?"

"I don't have a... phone," he said, stumbling on the word.

"You don't have a phone?" she echoed back, squeezing at her neck as she debated how she was going to get word to Liam. Knowing she was going to Mrs. Brennan's, he would probably expect her to be late coming back. The positive side to this was that he wouldn't be dispatching a search party for her, but that still didn't solve the problem of how she was getting back home.

Finn pulled out one of the high back chairs at the end of the table, and Kate sat on it, somewhat hesitant.

"Did I interrupt your dinner?" she asked, surveying the immaculate place settings. "I hope I didn't intrude, if you were expecting guests?"

"No," he said, his tone flat.

"Is your table always set up like this, then? It is... impressive."

"I guess," he answered, running his fingers through his hair.

"Do you live here alone?" She stared at him, aware of her own pang of jealousy behind her eyes. Up to now, she had never even wondered if he might not be unattached. He had kissed her after all, but did that really mean anything these days?

"I'm alone, yes. Don't feel sorry for me, it is by choice."

"Same here," she remarked, not feeling the need to go deeper.

"A hundred years is not too long to wait, if it is for the right one."

A slow steady creep of heat oozed through her body, and she looked down at the empty plate on the table, too afraid to meet his gaze. With her resistance already hanging by a thread, she felt sure she would be a goner if she did so.

With the tip of her pointer finger, she straightened one of the forks nestled on a neatly folded cloth napkin.

"Let me get you some tea," he said, "and we can get this all sorted out."

Too tired to protest, she melted back in the chair as Finn left the room, resting her heavy eyelids, and trying not to worry about failing to cross the bridge before dark.

A few minutes later, he returned with a tray. He pushed aside one of the place settings, clearing room to set it down, then poured Kate a cup.

Her attention was drawn to a large wooden breakfront along the wall that contained a beautiful burnished violin.

"Do you play?" he asked.

She couldn't help but flush at the way his head tilted once the question rolled off his lips.

"I do, actually. Well, I did. I've taken lessons since I was a child, but that is not to say that I am any good. I didn't even bother to bring my violin with me when I moved here, if that tells you anything. I hardly remember—"

Finn set the teapot down with a clatter and rounded the edge of the table. He picked up the gleaming instrument and moved toward her as if there was no time to lose. The next thing she knew, he was thrusting the violin and bow at her.

She released a little snicker, not at all sure if he was serious. The insistence in his eyes gave her pause, but before she could say anything, the violin was in her hand. She laid it across her knees and released a slow breath as she took it in. Finn held the bow out, so she accepted it from him, grasping hold of it at the frog. She twisted the screw and tightened the hairs, aware that it may not have been used in some time.

"What will you play?" He slid down into the chair to her left, leaning forward in clear anticipation.

"I know a few short tunes, or there is a longer one I could play? I probably wouldn't be able to do the whole thing without the sheet music, but it's one I have played many times. I could probably play a decent chunk of it, at least."

"Play the long one."

She smiled, giving him a gentle nod, finding his excitement almost adorable. "So, this one is a little deep, but it has always been one of my favorites."

"Deep?" He edged closer until his knee brushed against hers.

"It is a chaconne, by Johan Sebastian Bach. It is said that he wrote it in the depth of his grief for his wife after her death. Some say it touches upon every single emotion a person could possibly feel for another, but I suppose that is all just speculation. It is like Old Gus and his stories of the Good People."

He eased back, his eyebrows arched. "What do you mean?"

"Well… people like to add their interpretations to things. Spice up a good story to make it more interesting. Give context to things they can't quite understand. Bach was a true artist, and those types rarely have a quiet mind. The entire piece may have nothing to do with the depths of his emotions and was just a constant insistent melody he knew he had to compose. I will let you be the judge."

He sat straight. "Play it for me."

She threaded the bow across the strings, trying to recall all the notes she had played countless times. It had been such a long time since she'd attempted the piece, more an act of avoidance than anything. She liked to think of herself as a no-nonsense Kate, but deep down she knew that was only the top layer of the complexity that lay beneath. Music always had a way of bringing long-buried emotions to the surface.

As Finn watched her in anticipation, she had an almost deja vu feeling of being a young girl back at one of her first recitals. She began, fingering the strings with precision as she slid the bow. With deliberation, she kept her focus on the strings, a move that would have gotten her a firm reprimand from her old tutor back in the day. Now and again, she would look forward, out of sheer habit, and catch sight of Finn's wide eyes. He sat spellbound, as if her rusty playing was the most beautiful noise he had ever heard. She played as far as her memory would take her, then rested the violin back on her lap.

"I think Johan Sebastian Bach wrote that piece from a broken heart," he said.

Perhaps it was the way the light caught his eyes, but she could have sworn tears were welling. It felt wrong to pry, but something in her wanted to know.

"Why?"

"Can't you feel it in those notes? It's like being scattered in the wind. Play it again."

"Again? Finn, that's a rather long piece. Are you sure you want to—"

"Play it again."

She flinched at the insistence in his voice but acquiesced and laid the bow across the strings. As she made the first pull, she glanced up at him through her lashes. He sat there, anxious, awaiting each frame of the melody. His eyes were big and round, with all of his emotions laid out. She played better than before, perhaps for no other reason than to please him. It worked because the music seemed to bring out some long-buried joy in him. His usual matter-of-fact nature dissolved, replaced by something almost uninhibited.

In all honesty, he brought out the same thing in her. She barely knew him, yet there seemed to be no reason to guard herself against him. Maybe she should shy away from him, but the world appeared to have a different opinion. Time and again, they had been drawn to each other. It defied all explanations. She felt his energy, like a soft wind against her skin, and all his highs and lows pulsated through her veins, like a magnetic force pulling her in and pushing her away. There was no knowing what would come next. Being with Finn took her so far away from her troubles, she didn't want to ever turn back. It was like dwelling deep in the valley of indecision, far from everyone else, and being fully content with not being in control.

As she finished the chaconne, she looked up to catch his burning gaze fixed upon her face, his eyes as dark gray as storm clouds. For a moment, she was convinced that wherever they were now, it was somewhere only they knew.

"Could you feel it?" he asked, his voice soft, though she caught the barely perceptible crack that might have been missed by anyone else not as absorbed in him as she was.

"I felt it," she answered, setting the violin on the table. "All the sadness in the world. Like something was lost. Something that can never be again."

"What did you lose, Kate McCarthy?"

She swallowed hard, the lump in her throat refusing to budge. All of her inhibitions had faded, and she was left feeling like a patient on a therapist's couch. She wanted to tell him everything she had kept locked away for so long—to let go of all the instruments of self-destruction she had used against herself.

"I think I have always been lost, always waiting for some grand revelation that was never going to come. I'm a fraud, Finn. I have always been a fraud. I am the Lon Chaney of my age."

"Lon Chaney?" He blinked, and she knew the wheels in his mind were spinning.

She gave him the eye. "Don't you dare ask if he is my suitor."

His open mouth snapped shut.

"He is an actor," she continued. "The man with a thousand faces. Sometimes I feel a little like one of the monsters in his films. I'm a fraud. Smoke and mirrors. Like there is layer upon layer of stage makeup covering who I am. I muddle through life trying to give the impression that I am carefree, and can't be pinned down by anyone or anything but, inside, I know better. I am lonely, and I haven't accomplished anything worthwhile." She sat up. "I'm like the banshee. The bringer of misfortune. The harbinger of death and change." She held her open hand to her chest and took a steadying breath. "The only thing I have ever been good at is bringing bad luck to people. When I first came here, I felt like it was my second chance. Now I am not so sure."

"You don't like it in Ireland?"

"I love it here, actually. I love it here too much. Sometimes I think, if given the choice, I won't go back home. I just know myself too well, and it is only a matter of time before I wear out my welcome. There is no amount of change of scenery that will ever be enough, because it's me that won't change. I will be the same old Kate, Finn. My attention span for anything responsible is far too short."

"You could be happy here and not change who you are."

"Really? I am twenty-four years old, and don't have a lucrative job, not to mention that I have shot all my good marriage prospects to hell. I have single-handedly managed to alienate my family, and I am just about out of friends. People are tired of me, and I can't say I blame them. I am tired of myself. It is time for me to stop parading around like I have the world all figured out. I don't. Far from it, in fact. I want freedom, but need security. I want success, but hate the confines of coloring in the lines. I want far too much for what I am willing to give." She raised her brows and shrugged. "It just isn't working."

"Have you ever been in love, Kate?"

"No. Not really. I am not a good person, Finn. I don't give as much as I take. No one deserves to be loved by me. Why? Because I suck all of the light out of people. I become what they want me to be, but only for a time. I draw them in like a moth to the flame, then, just when they think they have gotten close, I decide it is too close and I slam the door shut. My conscience is like a room filled with ghosts, each one vying for center stage to take their revenge." She groaned inside, hoping he didn't hear it. "I have put so many people through the worst of me. It isn't fair to do it to another person."

"What would it really take to make you happy? What is that thing you are searching for that hasn't been found."

She stared down at her hands, trying to rein her emotional barrage back into check. Part of her wanted to tell him about her parents' visit, but the other part didn't want to think about it right now. Did Finn regret opening up these floodgates? She looked at him, surprised that he didn't look like a deer staring down two bright headlights. He seemed to be at ease. From her past experience, this sort of sensory overload would have been enough to send any other guy running out of the room screaming. Time to shift the attention from herself.

"Why is this all about me? I'm here at your dining table, baring my soul, and you haven't told me anything about you."

"What do you want to know?"

"Something. Anything that takes the spotlight off me for a second." Any shred of revelation would suit her. What was his favorite color? Did he like mushy peas? Did he have a dog as a child?

"Okay then. I am lonely too."

She waited, but nothing more came. The man was going to need prompting.

"I just let you into my deepest darkest places and that is all you're giving me? I do not think so. Cough it up. Tell me something juicy enough to share at the beauty shop, damn it."

He blinked twice, then nodded once. "I was separated from my family long ago. I have lived on my own since then. There was a time when I could have gone back, but I chose differently and the door closed."

"So, you don't want to go back, or it isn't an option?" Was his relationship with his family as fractured as her own?

"It is difficult to explain," he said.

"Thanks to my disabled transportation, I have all the time in the world." She followed this with a resigned sigh. "Take all the time you need."

He graced her response with a half-hearted smile, then pursed his lips, as if contemplating whether she was serious about his continuing. Something about his vulnerability sparked a surge of heat that filled her heart. He was altogether too glorious for words, perfect by design, yet flawed by his own choices. Just what those choices had been were yet to be revealed. Still, she sensed that they both shared a past each was trying to outrun. Like the chords of the chaconne she had played, some wordless melody told her there was an element left unfulfilled in him. Finn, like her, was also searching.

"When I first left," he said, "all I ever thought about was going back. It was the only thing I wanted." He leaned forward, resting his elbows on his knees and wringing his hands. "Then I met her. I thought there could never be another woman who would fill me with that kind of light. Everything was so different in the free world, so unlike anything I ever knew before. She didn't feel the same. I had some vision of what it could be like between us, but it never was to be. She released me, but there was nowhere else to go."

"You couldn't just go back home? Would your family not just forgive you for making a mistake?" She winced as the words came out, knowing well the hurt that came from feeling like you had wronged too many people to ever go crawling back. She had her own house of ghosts.

"That's the thing. I could have gone back, in the beginning. I would have never been faulted for things beyond my control. When she released me, she made me a promise. She told me that someday I would find exactly what I wanted. Someday, I would find the person who would make me forget all about her. I held onto that promise, and I knew that I couldn't go back and be happy until that was fulfilled. It could never be as it was before. I would never find a moment's rest, always searching for that person." He released a soft sigh, his right shoulder twitching in an almost-imperceptible shrug. "The hours and the days have dragged on since then. All this time, I have been searching for that someone. That one person who is going to fill this black cavernous void."

"Now we are getting somewhere," she said, struggling against the urge to hug him. She hated to think that his heart had been broken by another, when something in her wanted him for herself. "You want someone who completes you? You want all the cliché stuff that comes with love?" It sounded insensitive, but given her present discomfort it was the best she could do. Sarcasm had always been her security blanket.

"I want everything I just heard in that piece you played, Kate. All those highs and lows on a continuous loop. I want it stuck in my head for all my days. Our love story has no last chapter."

"Soft day, isn't it?" she said, squirming against her sudden unease.

He looked at her as if she had just sprouted wings and a tail. She focused on her watch and gave the glass a frantic tap.

"Dead," she muttered, throwing her head back in frustration. "I swear, I don't own anything that works." Her stomach gave out a low growl and, for a second, she eyed the beautiful tea tray he had prepared. This time, her hunger would have to take a sideline now she was on the cusp of tossing herself headfirst into Finn's love story. Every red flag waved in the wind as she inched her way into another bad decision. She needed an out, as soon as possible.

When she glanced out the window, all the light had faded from the sky, leaving nothing but her own reflection staring back against the dark backdrop.

"It has to be late. Liam will be worried if I don't return soon."

Finn's disappointment was evident as he got up and took the violin back to its place on the breakfront. He motioned for her to follow him, and led her to the front entrance. Once outside, he headed straight to the scooter. The isolation of Cahermann House made the night sky all the darker. With no lights from nearby houses to distort the view, Kate marveled at how the stars looked like thousands of tiny jewels glittering against a black velvet drape. It was obvious that, as much as she wanted to resist Finn and all his effortless charms, the gods were determined to conspire against her. Their treachery lay in the simplest of things: the teasing hint of burnt turf, the symphony of insects serenading them from their unseen hideaway, and the scatter of diamond dust against the ebony canopy above.

"Are you going out to the cliffs tonight?" he asked, crouching now on the far side of the scooter.

She considered it for a second. "No, probably not." As much as she wanted to spend more time with him, it wasn't a good idea tonight. He had a way of taxing her senses, in a manner that was sure to be her undoing. Funny he asked, though, because she hadn't been out for her usual nightly jaunt much as of late. It wasn't that she hadn't wanted to—the past few days had just been far too busy.

"Tomorrow night, then?"

She shrugged one shoulder. "Maybe."

"I see." He got up and kicked at some loose gravel.

"Are you going out to the cliffs?"

He looked at her. "I go out every night."

To date, he had made such a considerable effort to stumble upon her, now she felt herself needing to regain some sense of control. She wasn't sure what lay between them but it was speeding far too fast into an actual relationship—unlike any she'd experienced before. Things were not operating on her terms, and that gave her a growing sense of discomfort. Even if she was starting to like him more than she cared to admit, she needed to step back and regain her bearings.

"Then I know exactly where to find you if I want to see you, and where to avoid if I don't."

A sadness in his eyes played upon her sympathies.

"But the fresh air might do me some good. It all depends on how I feel. I am quite busy, you know."

His frown faded, replaced by the warmth of his perfect smile. It danced upon every one of her senses—her good sense most of all. She was quick to justify to herself that the confusion she'd been feeling of late was not infatuation for the god-like creature standing before her, but rather the fact she hadn't been out for those walks that had become such a nightly ritual. The night air always helped clear her mind. However, no matter what reasoning she threw at herself, his presence only complicated her every thought.

As if he could feel her urgency to break free from his spell, he lifted her helmet off the back of the scooter before returning to place it into her hands. Bewildered, she looked down at it, then back at him.

"It's broken down," she said, nodded to the pile of junk, wondering how he had already forgotten.

"Your scooter is fine. It was just out of petrol."

"Out of...?" She thought about it, not sure when she had bothered to refuel the tank. As she looked around, she wondered who had done it. Finn had no fuel can, and he told her he was here alone. An eerie shiver slithered down her spine, and for a brief moment, Old Gus's words about villains and gentleman trickled into her mind. Which one was Finn?

"There is petrol in the tank, now?"

"You are all good, Kate."

"But how? Who—" She stopped herself short as another wave of shivers gripped her. There was something in the way he stared back at her, offering nothing more in the way of explanation. It filled her with so many more questions but, somehow, she knew they wouldn't be answered.

She broke free of her jitters. "I guess I won't make it back over that bridge in time."

"What bridge?"

"Oh, it's just one of Old Gus's superstitions. He said I had to be over the Spectacle Bridge before nightfall. Apparently, Biddy Early warned about it a million years ago."

Finn's face took on a stonelike glaze. "Biddy said that?"

"Not you, too?" She huffed. "I will be fine. It is just a bridge."

He had already turned his head away, looking out into the night sky. She stood in silence as he surveyed the dark landscape, his hands stretched out, as if feeling a shift in the wind.

"I will get you back out onto the road. Then head straight home, do you understand? Stop for absolutely nothing."

She nodded her understanding, feeling like a timid child, aware that every hair on her body had risen, like Lazarus from the dead. While she was afraid, she wasn't sure of what. Finn? Biddy's warning about the bridge? All of this hocus pocus was weaving itself deep into her psyche. If she kept on listening to this nonsense, she was well on her way to becoming some babbling old superstitious recluse, scared of her own shadow.

As she drove back, she distracted herself by thinking about something more unpleasant than the bridge. Her parents' visit. Facing up to her behavior in Boston was difficult, but atoning for how she had treated them since was harder. She owned a healthy slice of this mess, and the only reason she didn't want to see them was because she knew she had to admit these wrongs. After pouring out her ugly side to Finn, she was a bit surprised at how much easier it was than expected. Being honest, even if unflattering, was quite freeing. Her mom and dad's trip here was proof enough that they also wanted reconciliation. Hope lay on the other side of that initial discomfort. They would all have to rip the bandage off and nurse their wounds. Once that part was done, things could resolve in their own time.

The upside to a resolution with her folks was that she might clear up the confusion in one area of her life. Finn, however, was adding more and more complexity with each passing day.

As she crossed over the bridge, she all but laughed out loud. Nothing. All that fuss for nothing.

She continued on her way, unaware of who watched her from the shadows. There, folded in the blanket of darkness, a rider sat on his horse. Beside them, on the grass, sat a beautiful woman, combing through long silky black hair, her amber-eyed gaze fixed on Kate McCarthy.

Chapter Eleven

T he inn was dark as she approached. She had no idea of the time, but it was far later than expected. After parking her scooter in its usual spot, she padded around the building until she reached her door. She turned the handle, careful to ease it open so its usual loud creak didn't wake the whole of Doolin. With no discernible light coming through the door or window, she held her hand out and waded into the room, trying to get her bearings in the darkness. When she reached the side of the bed, she knocked into the lamp. With cat-like reflexes, she caught it before it crashed to the floor, her heart skipping a beat. She righted it on the table, then pulled the dangling chain to switch it on, filling the room with a pale yellowish glow.

She threw her helmet onto the bed, swung around, and flopped down on the soft mattress. Her back hurt, the evidence of pushing the heavy scooter along the road settling low in her spine. She brought her knees right up and held them for a long exhalation, stretching the muscles out. Satisfied with that, she sat up, brought her hands to the side of her neck, and gave the aching muscles a much-needed squeeze. Then she stood up, ready to gather her nightclothes and put an end to the day. At her first step toward the dresser, she caught sight of something on the floor. She didn't need to move an inch closer, well aware of what it was. The comb's smooth wooden teeth were entwined in the rug's thick pile.

Her heart thundered in her ears like a galloping cavalry. All of a sudden, the room felt devoid of oxygen, with each breath stinging her lungs like a chemical burn. She scanned the space, back and forth, and while it was small, there was still the closet and washroom—even under the bed. The only weapon she found was a near-inoperable umbrella. Gripping it with both hands, she stalked across the floor, almost rolling her eyes at the thought that she could inflict damage on a waiting intruder with it. She released the snap around the cloth, debating whether she should open it. Why would you open it, you dummy? Use the wooden tip to jab them.

"Hello," she called out, thankful for the silence that returned, but no less uneasy. If someone were indeed hiding in her room, it was not as if they were likely to step out for a nice chat and offer her a plate of biscuits.

The bathroom door was ajar, and she shoved it open with the tip of the umbrella, then jabbed into the darkness. No response, which was a relief, but no way was she stepping in without the light on. She crinkled up her face and reached for the pull chain, gave it a swift tug, then pounced inside, umbrella ready for action.

Nothing. The space was empty.

She backed out and spun around to face the closet door. Not wanting to give her unwanted guest any indication of her movement, she tiptoed toward it, swallowing hard as she finalized the plan in her mind. As she curled her fingers around the heavy handle, her body felt as if it were boiling. Once again, she flung open the door, this time stabbing and jabbing the umbrella into the hanging clothes.

Nothing.

Given the pile of hangers and garments were now on the floor, she was confident she would have maimed anything lurking within.

The only place left was under the bed. This would be far more complicated. She wasn't excited about the prospect of coming face to face with her intruder but it had to be done. Gripping the umbrella like Arthur's Excalibur, she was about to go for it when she glanced over at the desk in the corner.

Perfect.

She switched the umbrella to her left hand and snatched up the full can of hairspray, then circled the end of the bed at a safe distance, careful not to come close to the comb. Using the tip of the umbrella, she eased up the bed's dust ruffle and, without further ado, emptied nearly the entire can under the bed. The room filled with the stench of pressurized alcohol, and she choked and coughed against the noxious fumes. Breath held, she crouched on her heels and took a look.

Nothing.

Aside from cloudy layers of hairspray, the space was empty.

She got up and let out a sigh of relief, forgetting her reality when she inhaled, being forced to cough and splutter out a lungful of lacquer. Then the object that incited all the panic caught her eye, and Seán's voice echoed in her head:

"It's the banshee's comb."

This time, she had no log grabber to pick it up. The room contained little more than she'd managed to bring with her from Boston. Still, she did not want to touch it, and surveyed her surroundings for something that might aid her dilemma. In the pile of mayhem that was once her tidy closet, lay a wire hanger. She picked it up, pondering just how she would get the job done.

She set the umbrella on the bed and stood over the offending article, pinching the end of the hanger between her thumb and forefinger. Then, she plucked at the comb until she freed its teeth from the carpet. With the thin metal of the hanger looped between two teeth, she eased it up, using the umbrella to hold it in place.

When she reached the door, she gasped. How the hell was she going to open it? Why hadn't she thought of that in the first place? She groaned, dropped the umbrella to the floor, angled her body so the comb stayed looped on the hanger, then twisted the door knob. But the damn thing started to wobble, and her hand trembled at the thought of dropping it. In a flash, she swung open the door and hurled the unwanted object out into the night. She didn't wait to hear it land, slamming the door shut and latching the inside lock. Next, she seized the chair from beside the desk and shoved it under the handle.

There, that should do it. No one or thing was going to get through that door tonight.

A thousand thoughts raced through her head, the most troubling being that someone or thing had invaded her personal space without her knowing. She never bothered to lock her door. There was no need. Doolin was by all accounts the safest place she had ever resided. Was this some joke? Some lame attempt to give her a good scare? It was widely known that she had never been receptive to the local lore, which she chalked up as antiquated beliefs—tales of fantasy meant to explain life's everyday snags. Something about the comb was different, though. And finding it on the floor wasn't an occurrence one could just dismiss. If this was the same comb from the pub the other night, then who felt the need to place it in her room? Who placed it in the pub the other night? Most of all, she couldn't wrap her head around why someone felt the tale of the banshee was so important for her to believe that they would go to such measures.

She considered all possible suspects. Old Gus was a well-respected man. Far too much of a gentleman to do such a thing. As a seanchaí, he held true to his own beliefs, and while he offered convincing arguments, he never sought to force his own opinions on others. If she believed his stories, fine, if not, then he still slept well at night. Seán, though prone to being a bit more passionate about the old ways, did not have a mean-spirited bone in his body. He might like a good verbal jab now and again, but he was far from the type to break into her room. It could have been one of the other workers at the inn, thinking a good practical joke would go down well. But she didn't have that type of relationship with any of them, not being there long enough or being the type to establish such a rapport. Besides that, she was the boss's relation. To trespass into her room was a bit of a stretch for anyone. They would know it wouldn't sit well with Liam and Edel.

Gripping the umbrella again, she scanned the room for any other clue that something had been moved, though she'd done such a good job of reducing it to a shambles, it was impossible to tell. If there was such a thing as a banshee, then a weapon a bit more intimidating than a broken umbrella would be needed. What could she use to fend her off? This may well be a question for the likes of Old Gus. Surely, he would have a list of things to keep the harbinger of death at bay. Her only hope was that, whatever he suggested, she could find it in one of the local shops. She would stockpile her arsenal, and grab a new can of hairspray while she was at it.

It took a good while for her pulse rate to settle back to normal. When her eyelids felt as though they couldn't stay open a minute longer, she slipped into her pajamas and got into bed. That night, she fell asleep sitting upright, umbrella clutched to her chest.

The next evening at the pub, Kate felt as if she hadn't slept a wink, though, in truth, she'd slumbered most of the morning away. Her sleeping habits had always teetered on the abnormal, but last night was rocky, to say the least, with her waking up many times, her nerves on edge. At some point, overcome with exhaustion, she fell into the deepest sleep she had in ages, and stayed shuttered up in her room for the day. When she did surface, to grab a quick bite to eat before starting her scheduled shift, she made sure to lock her door. She had never done it before, and it took a good deal of time to find the key Liam gave her when she first arrived. It was an inconvenience, but she wasn't about to subject herself to another night like that.

She hadn't bothered to check her reflection in the mirror, but imagined she looked like something resembling a walking corpse. Her eyes burned as though she had stared too long at the sun, the bags beneath them heavy like buckets of sand.

When she walked in, Liam was there, lost deep in whatever task was prominent on his mind, and didn't even glance up to see the shell of a human that approached. She gave a polite nod to Old Gus. If she had any doubts that she appeared haggard, the look of concern he returned made it clear. Desperate to break free from his unwavering stare, she moved behind the bar and took a freshly laundered apron from one of the shelves, ready to check the duty list for the night.

"I'm sorry I didn't get to see you last night when you got back," Liam said, leaning against the back counter as he took inventory of the bottles. "I saw your light on, but it was late and I didn't want to bother you. I trust everything went well with Mrs. Brennan."

He looked up from his pad of paper, awaiting her reply.

"Yes, she was feeling under the weather, but she sent her thanks." She pulled the apron strings around her waist. "Did you say my light was on when you passed by?"

"Yes." He looked at her, taking in her disheveled state for the first time.

"Funny." Her hands trembled as she looped the strings into a neat bow, and she took a short breath to steady herself.

"What is it, Kate?"

"It's probably nothing, but I was rather late coming home last night. My scooter had some mechanical trouble. By the time I got back, the whole place was dark, including my room."

He set his pen and paper on the counter and turned to her. "Did the bulb burn out?"

"It worked fine when I got back. I'm sure I turned the lamp off before I left." Again, she stalled, giving her lips a subtle pinch. "There was something else, though." She glanced around the pub. Only Old Gus and a few other patrons were within earshot. She stepped closer to Liam, not keen on letting everyone hear of her wild adventure with an umbrella as a means of defense against an empty room.

"I didn't notice it at first," she said, almost at a whisper. "It was wedged into the rug. If I didn't know better, I'd say it was the same comb I found on the floor here a couple of days ago. The one that Old Gus and Seán chucked out into the grass."

Liam's face remained still, but his eyes widened. "A comb, you say? You found one in the pub, then on the floor of your room last night?"

She responded with a simple nod, unsure if she sounded half crazy. Liam had known nothing of what happened the other night, so it took a second for everything to register.

Out of the corner of her eye, she saw Old Gus leaving the snug in the corner. For an old man, his hearing bordered on what one would call superb. Her attempt to keep the conversation between Liam and herself had failed. Ever wise to the mannerisms of those in his sphere, it looked like Old Gus had picked up on her reluctance to let him listen. Instead of coming over to her, he moved to an empty table nearby, no doubt expecting her to come over to him at some stage.

Had the incident not still haunted her, she doubted she would have brought it up with Liam. Part of her was embarrassed for allowing herself to be drawn into superstition and fanciful stories, while the other part was troubled at the thought that someone had been in her room. That had shattered her sense of security and could not just be swept aside.

"Do you recall if the door was locked when you left?" Liam asked, motioning for her to take a seat with him at the bar.

"I've never locked it before. I honestly never had a good reason to bother." She wet her bottom lip with the tip of her tongue. "Maybe it was James or one of the other girls playing a practical joke." She giggled, though it wasn't convincing. "I am always too quick to dismiss everyone's stories. Perhaps they thought it was high time I experienced one of my own. They probably thought they could make a believer of me." She didn't believe it for a second, but was desperate for a rational explanation.

"Aye, I wouldn't put it past them. I don't mind a good joke now and then, but within reason. Going into your room without you knowing was a step too far. I will ask around, just the same."

"I wouldn't want to accuse anyone," she added. "The whole thing just made me uneasy."

"I have some old iron door locks in the back shed. I will make a point to get one installed for you as soon as possible. I know the one you have will suffice, but a second wouldn't hurt. If anything, it will ease both our minds a little more"

"If it's no trouble?" She knew Liam always had an extensive list of things to do around the property. The inn was an old building, and always needed a repair or upgrade somewhere.

"No trouble at all." He leaned closer, his intention clear: that no one else would hear. "Lock the damn door, Kate."

"Oh, I've already started," she said, lowering her gaze to the floor like a recalcitrant child. If it wasn't a practical joke, what was the intruder's intention? Had the comb not been there, she probably wouldn't be any the wiser. That got her thoughts spinning all the more. Was this the only time? Did someone go in before? If the person was looking for something to take, they must have been disappointed. All of her worldly possessions amounted to little or nothing.

"Tell me, just how did you end up getting back here if your scooter broke down?"

She looked at him for a moment, sifting through the evening's sequence of events. "I had left Mrs. Brennan's only a short while before I heard a terrible sputter and it just up and died on the road.

Thankfully, it happened that I was out by Cahermann Hill. My friend Finn lives there. As luck would have it, he saw that I was having some trouble." She glanced over at Old Gus, aware that he was listening. No point saying anything about being in Finn's house. "Anyway, he helped me out and it fired right up, and I didn't have any problems after that."

Liam smiled as he nodded. Kate had been hesitant about mentioning Finn before, unsure of how her uncle might react. If anything, he seemed pleased, if for no other reason than she had been helped when in need.

With that out of the way, Liam gave her a short list of things to do before the pub got busy for the night. Her mind at ease, she hopped to her feet, eager to get started.

****

When Kate left to get her jobs done, Liam shifted in his seat and looked at Old Gus for a long moment. The seanchaí gave a knowing nod in return.

"I'd say that iron lock is well in order," he said. "It will keep her out. She won't go near iron."

Liam responded with a firm nod, running through the details of Kate's story. He raised an eyebrow. "Any idea who this Finn chap is with a house out on Cahermann Hill?"

Old Gus remained quiet for a moment, cupping his chin in one hand. "There isn't a house out on Cahermann Hill." He moved his hand to the back of his neck and gave it a sharp squeeze.

Liam knew he'd lived in this part of Clare most of his life, and there wasn't a person or place he didn't know by heart.

"Only thing out there is an old fort. A fairy fort, to be precise."

Chapter Twelve

As she leaned back in the chair at her dressing table, Kate gave herself a onceover. She wasn't stunning by any means but, in reality, it was 2 a.m., and any attempt at glamming herself up would be lost in the darkness. She'd met Finn out along the pathway to the cliffs nearly every night for the last week, and her late-night excursion had become the thing she looked forward to most each day.

She eased the door shut behind her, locked it, then slid her arms into the sleeves of her cardigan. The heat of the summer day had dissipated, giving way to a cool coastal breeze. Flashlight in hand, she headed out to their meeting place, smiling to herself as she traveled the familiar path. Somewhere in the course of the past few days, she had stopped scolding herself for being attracted to Finn. There was such an easy comfort between them. She flipped back through the pages of her mind, recalling each and every relationship she'd had through the years. The list wasn't long, with most of them being short-lived. Finn was the first person who made her feel like there was no reason to be anything but herself. Even when he teased her for her sharp tongue, he never so much as hinted at not liking her wit. In truth, it was the opposite with him. If he was anything, he was tenacious, and that extended to matters of the heart too. He did not shy away from a challenge, and she doubted he could be fully content with someone who was meek and mild.

Just the thought of him warmed her body at its core. Somehow, in the midst of the most-chaotic phase of her life, she had managed to stumble upon, literally, the single most-perfect person. There was no point in keeping her distance. Even if she stopped now, spun around and headed home, vowing to never see him again, she couldn't turn back emotionally. She was already too far gone, having fallen head over heels for Finnley, and her heart was far too full to allow any space for logic.

A few minutes later, she watched the slow steady saunter of the stallion as it moved across the horizon. She remained seated on the boulder, not ready to leave the shroud of shadows. Perhaps it was the voyeuristic element, but something in her wanted to observe Finn undetected. Everything about him was intriguing—even strange—which is what held her attention.

Even in the darkness, he possessed a certain brilliance. His outline, perched high atop the horse, was strong and confident. A man of mystery. Intoxicating, like the sweetest daydream that is never quite finished. Watching him gave her such a thrill, and she shuddered at the icy ripple it sent through her.

The subtle cloud cover parted, giving him an ethereal silhouette. He turned his head toward her, and eased back on the reins when he spotted her tucked away in her safe haven. She was unsure whether to credit the flash of heat spreading through her to embarrassment for being caught watching him, or something else.

Step by step, he moved closer, his approach drawing the air from her lungs. In no recent nor distant memory could she recall ever being so off-balance. Finn had some wordless way of setting all the world in motion, but leaving her standing still. A part of her still loathed this giddiness welling up in the pit of her stomach, and wanted to claw away the uncontrollable smile that cursed her lips as he came close enough for her to make out every one of his glorious features.

She was far too smart to be smitten by good looks, or to bask in this nameless euphoria, like some junior high school girl who just received her first love note. However, all her wisdom and experience aside, her penchant for needless recklessness was hard to suppress. He had edged his way into her heart, making her feel as if nothing, save some catastrophe of epic proportions, could undo what was already done.

He greeted her with a boyish grin as he pulled up, and it was damn near her undoing. After sliding from the saddle, he gave the stallion a few soft strokes along its neck. In that moment, she imagined him scooping her up and pressing his lips against hers, like some dark villain. She would have put up a fight for two solid seconds, with about as much resistance as she could muster before letting herself melt into every last inch of him. Before he turned to her, she raised her fingers to her lips, trailing along their softness, savoring the heat of that imaginary kiss.

When he looked at her, she was glad he couldn't read the thoughts swirling through her idiotic head. A ragged breath caught in her throat as he stepped forward and sat in the grass at the base of her boulder. He leaned to the side and rested his arm against the rock, so close, his shirt sleeve brushed against her denim-clad leg. She sat as stiff as an old oak beam, fighting her inclination to scoot over and give him room.

"How did you know I was here?" she asked, trying to disguise the way he overloaded her senses.

"I can always see you, Kate. Plus, your flashlight is lying right there on the ground. It's kind of a dead giveaway."

"Oh, I could have sworn I switched it off." She reached down to retrieve the lit torch from the grass.

"Keep it close. Walking out here in the dead of night without it is a bad idea."

"We already came to that conclusion," she said. "As I recall, we agreed it was unlikely that I would heed any attempt at a reasonable warning."

"Yes, we did, but I thought you might think it over and decide I was right after all."

"If you thought me logical, then you were gravely mistaken. I shy away from anything that requires good sense."

"Then I guess I should be grateful for your obstinacy. Otherwise, I would be out here all alone." He followed this with a halfcocked grin.

"I have walked these trails many times, and I have only been run over by a man on a horse once. I consider those to be fairly good odds."

"Did I run you over? As I recall, it was you who was in my way."

"We have different recollections of that night. I think it is safe to say we can agree to disagree."

"You haven't been in Ireland very long," he stated. "You will find there is more to fear than me out in the darkness. Everything about this land is different when night falls."

She could hardly disagree with that observation. He got up and moved further into the darkness. For a moment, she sat still, letting her mind become detached as she scanned the brilliance of the stars hovering above.

"What is it that you think about out here all alone?" he asked from somewhere off in the distance.

"All the things I try desperately to wash from my mind." She shifted on the boulder. "I broke someone's heart."

"A girl like you is bound to break a heart or two in your lifetime."

She scanned the darkness until she picked up his silhouette lowering onto the grass. Next, he was lounging on his back, staring up at the glistening firmament. Without a word, she moved to his side and lay beside him to do the same.

"Men fight differently than women, Finnley. I bet a good jab or two and you can walk away satisfied. I am not happy until I have thoroughly crushed the man's soul."

"It can't be all that bad," he said, his subtle laugh betraying his amusement.

"Oh, it was. I refused a marriage proposal. In front of thousands of people. It is a sure-fire way to render anyone a sworn enemy."

"Do you know why I love stars?" he asked after a few seconds of silence.

"Because they are just so damn pretty?" she offered, easing her hands behind her head like a makeshift pillow.

"There is that," he agreed. "I think I like knowing that there are so many things bigger than me. Things that cannot ever be explained. Things I won't ever understand."

"That kind of frustrates me." She snickered. "I have this relentless need to know everything about everything. Why on earth do you want to be confused?"

"Life can be so hard. Things happen, and you beat yourself to death trying to figure out why. That sky." He pointed at it. "It gives me hope. I like knowing that my problems are so small compared to the bigger mysteries of life. I like knowing that some questions will never be answered. Some things will never be understood. It helps me know that sometimes we don't have to close every door to move on. It is okay to just live life, even without knowing all of the whys."

She nodded to herself. "Hmmm…"

"You don't agree?"

"No, that makes perfectly good sense, but I think I could better appreciate the philosophical depth of that statement if my brain wasn't absolute mush. The pub was packed tonight."

Finn released an audible breath, following with a soft chuckle. "You are exhausted and here I am rambling on about life's great mysteries. I guess it is a little heavy of a topic for tonight."

"I am tired, to be sure, but don't stop pondering the universe on my account. It's kind of nice to take a break from real life and just live in the moment. I certainly don't do it as well as I should."

"No one ever does," he said. "It is too easy to get lost in ourselves. We are born with everything we need. All the answers to every question are in us, if we just take the time to pay attention."

She rolled onto her side and propped her head on her hand. "I think that's one thing you and I don't actually agree on, Finn. I personally don't think I have any answers."

In response, he gave her a sideways smile. "You are looking with your eyes, trying to make sense of what you see. The answers are in what you don't see."

"My, do you ever sound like Old Gus right now." She eased back down to rest her head on the grass.

"Maybe he knows more than you give him credit for."

"You are probably right on that point," she conceded. "Old Gus is wise. He has spent his whole life studying people, and believes that nothing happens by chance. Everything and everyone is part of some intricate web. To him, it is all about figuring out the purpose fate has in mind."

"Exactly."

"That sounds all well and good, but I fail to see how I managed to get to this point in my life. I definitely am not following the plan."

"Did you have a plan?"

The note of seriousness in his voice gave her pause. She'd never really had a plan, always hoping she would luck out and just fall into her destiny without much effort.

"I think you already know the answer to that question," she said. Even if she didn't have an actual plan for her life, her pride was still a bit bruised at her omission. "I'm not where I thought I would be, but I can't say I am not happy with where I am."

His warm hand wrapped around hers, and she smiled when he gave it a gentle squeeze.

"Things are exactly as they should be, Kate. A plan would not have made any difference."

"So, you and I are supposed to be lying here in the grass, at this very moment, looking up at the stars? All the messiness in life was to lead us here to this particular spot?"

"Precisely," he said, holding her hand a little tighter.

She didn't say anything, but she felt something resembling a nervous tremble in his grasp. Perhaps it was selfish, but she liked knowing he was just as unsure as her.

"Even if you don't believe it," he continued, "I was meant to stumble upon you the night we met. It could only have been you. You were meant to travel all this way to turn my world around. You were sent to wreck my heart in all the best ways, and if I am not being too bold, I think you have done your part a thousand times over."

She blinked, letting the air gather in her lungs in a slow satisfying burn. If all of nature had conspired to bring her to this moment, then who was she to argue? She had never felt so alive. All her days leading up to meeting Finn had felt so gray, devoid of color. As she peered up at the inky sky, all the hidden hues appeared. Finn brought so much wonder to her world, stripping away the blanket of gloom she had burrowed herself into for so long. If she'd somehow managed to do the same for him, it was purely by accident. She never knew herself to be anything but misfortune to others. If ever she had brought good to anyone, those moments felt few and far between.

There were so many things she wanted to say, but no one sentence could tap into the emotions she was struggling to unpack.

"What do we do now?" It was the best she could manage.

Finn remained silent for a long moment, his own thoughts taking their sweet time. He released his grip on her hand, rolled onto his side and cupped her chin. As he stared down at her, his lips curved into a wide smile, then he brushed a few of her wily curls back from her cheek.

"To hell with any of the plans you and I ever had, Kate. Whatever we thought we were destined to do, was wrong. You and I are fate's plan."

She wanted to shout out that she damn sure liked fate's plan better, but before she could utter a word, his lips were on hers. If this kiss was the first phase of the new plan, she was one-hundred percent on board. She eased her eyes shut, cloaking her world in sheer darkness, but only for seconds. As she grazed her fingertips along his back, memorizing every curve, each of her senses awakened—her mind flashing with color, her skin electrified. The coolness of the night was replaced with a swift rush of heat, their breaths mixing together in a symphony, his kiss tasting like pure indulgence.

He wrecked her in all the best ways, too. The man was her undoing, shattering her heart into fragments, more numerous than all the stars above. She had sworn to herself she would never be here, ready to fall. For all the shoring up she had done against her emotions, it was no match for the likes of Finn. With silky ease, he had maneuvered his way past all her defenses, and with little effort, he'd found all the hidden spaces – the softest parts of her soul. She gripped the fabric of his shirt as his kiss deepened. All the work she had done to protect her unpredictable heart was done. Now, she was heading into uncharted territory, and there was nothing left to do but hold on.

Chapter Thirteen

When Kate opened her eyes, her sight fixed on the starry night pushing its way through the open drapes. She'd been too lazy to close them before crawling into bed, but that was hardly the reason to be awake at this late hour. A busy mind often prevented her from getting a good night's sleep. And while her worries drained her enough to be tired, that was usually short lived. She would awaken to pick up right where she left off, replaying all the things that couldn't be changed, as if some hidden answer would surface out of the blue.

It was 4 o'clock on Friday morning. By now, her mom and dad were preparing to depart on their flight. Crossing an ocean and a time zone, they would arrive in Dublin come late afternoon. From there, they would no doubt take an hour or two to recoup from the journey, grab a bite to eat, then hop in their hired car for the trip to Doolin. The journey would take several hours, and with any luck, they might encounter some sort of delay along the way.

Liam figured they would arrive at the inn well into the evening, giving her some shred of hope that she might skate by one more day before seeing their faces.

Prolonging the inevitable was bittersweet. On one hand, it offered her more time to get herself prepared. On the other, it just added to her already unbearable anxiety. The more she thought about this reunion, the more indecision bubbled up. No matter the outcome of their visit, she wasn't ready to leave this place that had so quickly become like home. Most of all, she wasn't ready to leave Finn, but she couldn't tell her family about him yet. Even if she hadn't fully decided where their relationship was going, she had no desire to cut it off either.

If she could prove that her time in Ireland had been productive, that she had grown, and was no longer the wild-spirited girl they'd sent away, they might consider letting her stay on a bit longer. It was an optimistic wish, but not one she considered reality.

As much as she wanted to convince her parents that she was different, she knew it wasn't the case. It would take far more than a few months in Ireland, or any other place in the world for that matter, to change Kate McCarthy. There would always be a wild wind flowing through her, threatening to veer her off any preset course. Finn was right. From the day she set foot on Irish soil, she hadn't bothered to make any sort of plan. She was only living for the moment, adapting to her surroundings, and reveling in the freedom of it all. In truth, she had spent more time doodling in her sketchbook than considering her future.

She worked through her usual list of self-flagellations, blaming herself for everyone else's displeasure, and convincing herself that all the world's problems rested solely on her shoulders. When at last she was satisfied she'd punished herself enough with mental lashings, her rebellious nature peeked out from the shadows. Every bit of unhappiness she'd ever felt—each punch of disappointment—had never really been her own. She was not unhappy with herself. All of her so-called mistakes were branded as such by others. Failing to get a degree in something she did not like wasn't a mistake on her part, and the world did not end because she refused to marry a man she didn't love. True, her decisions inconvenienced people, but she only did what was right for herself. Now that Finn had come into her life, she was sure she'd made the right call back in Boston.

One thing she always believed was that life gave everyone a finite number of days. There was no greater travesty than to waste them, for not one would ever be returned. Because of that, she could not justify squandering this treasure and living unhappily. She was twenty-four years old, well capable of making her own choices, and no longer beholden to her parents for direction. If she wanted, she could stay here in Doolin and work her dead-end job in the pub for as long as she pleased. She did not need her parents' permission to do so. Yes, they believed the opposite, but she could pack her bags and go back to Boston if she wished, or anywhere in the world, to do anything she wanted, with no accountability for her choices but to herself. Her parents needed to understand this, though she wasn't oblivious to the fine print.

If she truly wanted her independence, she had to be prepared for all that entailed. She couldn't just sever the strings of her choosing. True independence meant total self-reliance, which was necessary considering she would no longer expect financial support from her parents, or look upon them as her safety net when she stumbled. She never considered herself to be overindulged; the family's means were not so vast to extend outrageous luxuries upon their only daughter. Yet, she'd never gone without, well into her adulthood. However, breaking those ties meant growing up in every sense of the word. There was gravity in that commitment, and how her parents might perceive her desire to break away was still up in the air. It was possible they would embrace it. Maybe it was something they'd wanted for a while. Though, relinquishing their long-held control over a daughter unable to stay on the right path for long might prove more difficult than they imagined. Only time would tell how either she or her parents fared, but the need for change was prevalent.

For the first time since learning of her parents' plan to visit, she felt herself relax. As she worked through how she would present the news, a palpable sense of peace washed over her. It was odd, this feeling of complete control over her own decisions. She'd never had the good fortune of being confident in her choices, but now, all her pent-up bitterness dissolved, along with her worry and the insecurity of feeling like a failure. Was this the way responsible people felt all the time?

After a night of fragmented sleep, the morning came too soon. Well, maybe notions of it being morning was pushing it. By the time she rose, washed up and got ready, afternoon tea was wrapping up in the inn's parlor. This was a late start even by her standard. Having filled a plate with some leftover sandwiches, she hovered over a tiered dish of delicate cream puffs in the shape of a swan. A quick scan of the room revealed only a few remaining guests who were finishing up, so she dropped two of the pastries on her pile and tucked herself away at a table in the corner. One of the best perks of working at Doonagore House was having access to the leftover food from breakfast, lunch, and the evening tea service. It was rare that she ever needed to provide her own meals.

She nursed her first cup of tea of the day, staring out the window at the golden glow of a warm summer sun. The horizon held great change—she could feel it in her bones. She flipped up the top layer of a sandwich to survey its contents, pleased to see cucumber and tomato atop some sort of white spread. It took no time to devour nearly half of it at once.

Her excitement was growing at the prospect of feeling like an adult for the first time in her life. To her surprise, she found herself looking forward to her parents' arrival. In her head, she had rehearsed all the words she planned to say, until it felt as if they might roll off her tongue with no effort. Taking control of her own destiny was exhilarating, but as she scooped up another sandwich, she peered down at those waiting cream puffs. Soon, she would need to secure her own place to live, and these little delicacies would be a thing of the past. The thought of being responsible for herself was daunting, yet she understood it as part of the process.

She was determined to stay in Ireland, at least for as long as she could manage. Her parents may not be enthusiastic about the idea—an unintended consequence of sending her here—but returning to Boston just didn't feel right at the moment. She wanted to give herself a real shot at making this work. Was her meager pay at Doonagore House enough to survive, or would she have to seek employment elsewhere? On the face of it, that wouldn't be too difficult, but she couldn't deny that her skill set was somewhat limited. She pondered the type of employment she was qualified to obtain. Though she preferred to stay in Doolin, there weren't a lot of options in a small rural community, and a move closer to a town or city might offer more opportunity for better pay. Budgets and numbers swirled through her mind until the steady creep of insecurity threatened her recently mended frayed edges.

It was far too beautiful a day to soil with all those details so she swept the logistical part of her newfound adulthood to the side. Besides, she had no doubt that once she spoke to her parents, they would poke plenty of holes in her plan, giving her a far greater list of things to consider. Whether she wanted them to or not, they would offer an ample amount of guidance on the matter.

Just as she nibbled the head off the last of the sugary swans, Liam passed by the parlor door and made his way to her table, pulling up a chair to her left.

"Heard from your dad early this morning," he said. "There was a bit of a hiccup with the Dublin flight."

She struggled to keep her reaction from her eyes, not sure what was worse, her disappointment, or the hint of relief. "They aren't coming?"

"Oh, they are, they are. They will be here today, just a bit later than planned. Their plane will land in Shannon Airport instead. I suspect by the time they drive here, it will be quite late, and they will be well worn from the journey." He nodded once, tapping the back of her hand. "Best to expect to see them tomorrow morning."

She laughed. "I can tell by your face that, when you say *morning*, you are insinuating before noon."

"You read me well," he said, his smile lighting his eyes up. "I never mind your sleeping hours, much. You working the late shift means I actually get to bed at a decent hour for the first time in years. What time you go to bed or what time you rise in the afternoon is your business, but I figured you might want to make an exception for tomorrow."

Her emotions were mixed. She had started looking forward to seeing her mom and dad. These past three months felt like ages. The delay was just a few hours but disappointing just the same.

She was scheduled to work that evening, but Liam had arranged for someone to cover her shift, thinking they might all enjoy a welcome dinner when her parents arrived. Now, with the change in plan, she suggested that she might as well work. If anything, it would pass the time. Liam agreed, saying he would fix it.

As he left, she peered past the blush-pink lace curtains, toward the sea. She had promised Finn she would meet him out on the cliffs tonight. Given that she needed to be up in the morning, she would have to be mindful of her time. Her lax schedule was another aspect of her life that would undergo significant change. She looked down at her watch, the one that never seemed to work when she needed it to, and gave it a good winding.

Her lips warmed with the memory of Finn's kiss last night. He'd left her so shaky in herself, she barely remembered walking home. She stuffed the remaining bits of the cream puff into her mouth, aware that her heart, much like her stomach, gravitated toward things that were unhealthy. Like the way one delights in a handful of cookies or chips, but never a good stalk of celery. Any rational adult could see that this was poor timing for a relationship, considering the disarray in her life, and her self-induced rebirth as an adult didn't mean she had achieved a solid grip on wisdom just yet.

It was safe to say she liked him. No, it was far more than like but she hesitated to use the other word. Finn was so different from anyone she had known in the past. The way the thought of him evoked such a physical effect on her body was proof enough, and to say she enjoyed his company was an understatement. She was already counting down the minutes until tonight. And why not? She loved the way he tapped into the spirited side of her, not wanting to stifle it as others always had. He was fun and witty, always keeping her on her toes, pushing back when she wanted to best him. It dazzled her the way he could be reserved and vulnerable at the same time, and how he let the softer side of himself come up for air at the right moment. There was still so much she didn't know about him, because much of him remained mysterious, keeping her ever guessing, drawn by the need to know more.

Chapter Fourteen

At the beginning of her shift, Kate was surprised to see Old Gus already seated in his cozy spot in the snug, a fresh cup of tea pressed to his lips. It was Friday night, and she rarely saw the likes of him or Seán, as they usually headed out to whoever was hosting the session that week. She watched the old widower as he stared out the little window at his side. There was a lonesomeness in that, his quiet contemplation. From the day she'd arrived in Doolin, she knew him as Aonghas Clune—Old Gus, the seanchaí—the equivalent of a local rockstar. Never had she bothered to consider that, beneath all that, he was just a lonely old man, seeking to fill his idle time. Sharing his stories—ones he'd spent half his lifetime researching and retelling—was his means of escape from the hurt of his loss.

In that moment, she considered herself a bit selfish for always balking at his tales. As she approached him, his gaze remained fixed on the distant view or memory out the window, and that brought her to a halt. This was Gus's moment, not one she ought to invade. She was about to turn on her heel when he broke free from whatever held his attention and greeted her with his trademark grandfatherly smile.

"Tell me some more about Biddy Early," she said. Her words were as unexpected to herself as they were to Old Gus. She couldn't help it, needing to do something to help release whatever memory held him hostage. His eyes lit up as if he had just won a prize.

"Where do I even begin?" he said. "There is so much to tell." He gestured for her to sit at the table. "Biddy Early was born in seventeen ninety-eight, in a village south of here called Faha. Little is known about her early life, except her parents died when she was quite young, and she was raised in the workhouse. She died in eighteen seventy-four."

"That would have made her seventy-six," Kate said. "A good long life for those days."

"Those were very tough times indeed. Money was hard got, and illness knew no stranger. She was married four times, and outlived all of her husbands. She was known as one of the best herbalists—a healing woman. People would travel miles upon miles to seek out one of her remedies. You have to remember, these were very poor people, living through the years of the blight—the Great Hunger. There was no money for doctors as there is today."

"She must have earned a sizable living, though. I'm sure she was paid for her services in some way."

Old Gus sat back in his chair and gave a deep-rooted laugh, slapping his knees with glee. "That's the thing about it. In terms of her income, Biddy was what most would call a peasant woman until the day she died. She never asked for anyone to pay. If you wanted to give her something, she would accept it, but never once did she ask for a thing. It was said that her house was always stocked with eggs and plenty of poitín."

"Didn't you say she was a well-known bean-feasa—a wise woman—a seer of the divine? Maybe it was just all that poitín talking."

"I imagine she partook in a swig or two. The women of Clare were not exactly her biggest fans. You see, Biddy and her husband of the day were always willing to share a drink or two with their visitors. As a wise woman, she got herself into trouble with the likes of the clergy. Biddy was well known for her predictions, this is true, but her sight didn't stop with our world. She could see the Good People just as well. Biddy could tell your name and why you had come, without a word from your mouth."

A shiver ran across Kate's shoulders. "Biddy could see the Good People? What did she see?"

"She was on the best of terms with them. It is said that she had in her possession a small blue glass bottle—a gift from the Good People. When she peered into this bottle, she could see well into the future."

"Whatever happened to the bottle? After she died, I mean."

"No one really knows. Believe me, I know a great many people who have scoured her house there in Feakle looking for it. If anyone ever found it, they have never said."

"Her house still stands?"

"It's little more than an old shell—not much left of it now—but it is still there, tucked away in a wooded grove on the outskirts of Feakle. There is an old legend that speaks of a curse that will befall anyone who removes anything from the site that doesn't come from the earth."

"Well, she was an herbalist after all. I suppose she wouldn't be opposed to someone taking a plant or a flower, especially if it was meant for healing."

"I put no stock in those legends. Biddy was a good woman. She lived her entire life to serve others. She may have been a thorn in the side of the clergy, and the local law was never on her side, but she had no fear of them, being there to help people. She wasn't the type to bring harm upon anyone, unless she felt it was in good order."

It was clear that Old Gus held a reverence for the woman. He never hesitated to speak on her wit and talents as a bean-feasa. Back in Biddy's time, a hair brain like Seán might have spoken out against her and her like. Seán was a follower, easily swayed by superstitious rubbish and prone to believing popularly held opinion. Old Gus was different; perception was never reality to him. He dug well beyond the surface level.

"She sounds quite rebellious. Not a woman to stay quiet and out of the way."

"I suspect that you and Biddy would have had much in common, Miss McCarthy. Neither of you are very good at staying in the lines. Biddy had no qualms about teaching a good lesson to anyone who didn't treat her kindly."

"Back to the Good People," she said, wanting to steer the seanchaí's wandering mind back on track. "Could she talk to them?"

"I like to think so. It only makes sense, considering that is where she got the blue bottle. Most of all, Biddy was keen on when someone brought the wrath of the Good People upon themselves. If you followed what she told you to do, you could undo your wrong, but only if you followed her directions precisely. I mean, not one step could be missed. There were a great many people helped by her wisdom. So many that no one, save the clergy—mad because she cut into their spoils—doubted Biddy had real power."

Kate crossed her legs at the ankles, resting her elbow on the table. "How exactly does one anger the Good People?"

"Sometimes it is intentional, but I gather most of the time it is just ignorance. Interfering with a fairy path is a good way. Entering into a fairy fort, without their permission. Trespassing into their space is quite serious to the Good People."

"Tell me more about these fairy forts." She leaned in closer, maintaining hard eye contact.

"Egghead scientists would call them bronze age ring forts. They estimate there are at least forty thousand scattered across Ireland."

"Wait..." She tilted her head to the side. "Are those the circular stone mounds I see everywhere?"

"Yes, indeed." He paused to sip his tea, releasing an appreciative sigh. "We Irish know well that those are the homes of the fairies. Many have told of hearing music long into the night coming from the forts. Fairies love music, and especially love to dance. There is an old tale of a girl who wandered into a fort. She had heard the music and was curious. The fairies wouldn't let her go until she danced with them. She danced so long that her toes fell off."

Kate cringed as she visualized the scene. "So, they held her captive?"

"Anyone who enters may well find themselves trapped in the fairy world for as long as they want you to be. That is not to say someone they take favor upon might be able to leave of their own accord. It is entirely up to them. I have heard stories of farmers whose livestock won't even enter them. Animals have a sense about such things."

"Tell me, Old Gus, how does one protect themselves from the Good People?"

The old man glanced toward the bar. "They won't go near iron. A black-handled knife is a good deterrent too. Running water is another of their weaknesses. Remember when I told you about Spectacle Bridge? Now you know why."

Kate nodded to herself as his words sank in.

"Biddy used to speak of a black dog that awaited unsuspecting travelers at the entrance of a bridge. It was a big brooding beast—an omen of very bad things. Nightfall is the most dangerous time. It is the time when the fairies, both good and bad, are on the move. The dog lies in wait, hell bent on keeping its prey from crossing that bridge. You see, they cannot cross over running water."

Kate shuddered, thinking back to how Finn's demeanor had changed when she'd mentioned Old Gus's warning of the bridge. Perhaps he, too, put stock in such tales. She had crossed without incident, though. Even laughing at what all the fuss had been about.

"Samhain is the most dangerous time of all," Old Gus said. "It is when the veil between our world and theirs is thinnest."

"We call it Halloween back in Boston. The night when everyone dresses up in spooky costumes and tries to scare the living daylights out of each other."

"Yes. Don't you even think about going out for one of your walks on the cliff that night," he warned, his tone leaving no room for dissention.

"I promise," she said, though it was just the beginning of August and she doubted she would even remember his warning by then, if she were still here.

"Did I ever tell you the story of the farmer and the horse?"

"I have heard a good many stories," she replied, "but I don't recall that particular one."

"If you want to know what Biddy was all about, then this is the story for you. You see, there was once a farmer who owned a horse that had been struck with terrible sickness. Now these were different times, as I said, money was hard got, and to lose an animal as valuable as a good horse could spell absolute disaster. Well, this farmer went out to see Biddy. He waited all day in the queue, and finally it was his turn. There was Biddy standing at the old half door to her cottage. He didn't have to tell her his name, for Biddy always knew who you were and what you were about before you even got there. Still, she let him tell his story, and when he finished, she thought about it for a moment.

"Why did he even need to tell his story, if she already knew what he was going to say?"

Old Gus's brows furrowed. "It was common courtesy. I am sure the fella traveled a good distance."

Kate nodded. "Yes, that makes sense."

"Well, Biddy thought about it for a while and then she told him just what he should do. She said, 'Go back home, and when you get there, you will find that your son has taken ill too. At the stroke of midnight, your child will awaken and sneeze three times. On the third sneeze, you must say "God Bless you." If you do, your child will live but the horse will die. If you do not say the words, then your horse will live and the child will die.'"

"What a perfectly dreadful story," Kate exclaimed in shock. "I thought Biddy was about giving people cures. Why would she ever prescribe such a thing?"

"One thing you should know about Biddy is that she always gave people the choice. That choice didn't necessarily mean it was an easy one. Not all of our destiny is meant to be rosy. Life's lessons are not to be changed, and sometimes there is beauty in darkness."

Kate fought the urge to grimace. "I see no beauty in the prospect of a child dying."

"Let me continue, and I think you will see what I am getting at here."

"Oh, go on then."

"Well, the farmer returned home, and there he met his wife at the door. You can imagine that she was anxious to hear what Biddy had said. Bear in mind this was the farmer's second wife, stepmother to the young boy. Well, after he recounted his story, he was very torn at what his choice would be. If he lost that horse, it would spell financial ruin for the family. He, his wife, and son might well die of poverty and starvation at the end of it all anyway. The thought of that ripped him to shreds. He knew that Biddy's advice must be followed precisely. Despite all his doubt, his wife was resolute—she had come to love the boy as her own—in her eyes, the horse was the one to go."

"That is rather rare in a story," Kate said. "It's not often that you hear of a loving stepmother. It is a refreshing change, if I do say so myself. I am glad she had good sense." She stopped herself, eager to know the end of the story. "Go on, Old Gus."

"Well, the husband and wife barely spoke the rest of the night. Just as Biddy said, the child had come down with a sickness and it got worse by the minute. Then, at midnight, when all the rest of the world was asleep, they heard a sneeze. Just as Biddy had directed, they said nothing. Then the second sneeze, and still nothing. When at last they heard the third sneeze, the wife looked up at her husband. 'God bless you,' he said."

"Oh, thank heavens," Kate cried, the words coming on a breath she'd held a bit too long.

"Well, the next morning, the horse was dead as a doornail. Though the child was still ill, he eventually made a full recovery to health. Now, you might have thought that the farmer would be ruined, but the wheel of fortune soon turned in his favor. Over the next year, he was so blessed with such good fortune that he ended up far better off than he had ever been."

Kate nodded. "If he had chosen the horse over the child, it may have been quite different."

"Only Biddy would have known. You see, Biddy could show you the ways to help your problem, but she never told you which was the right one. She left it up to you to decide. If you choose the right way, then you might find yourself blessed with far more than you could imagine. When I say she was a good woman—the finest of women—I don't say it lightly. Biddy understood that you can only interfere with fate up to a certain point. At some stage, you have to face the fact that, like it or not, some things are just meant to be the way they are, and it isn't our place to change them."

The pub was slower than usual this evening, and Kate couldn't help but glance up at the clock. Old Gus had gotten so lost in his story, it was well past the time he would have normally left. "It's Friday," she said, as a gentle nudge. "Aren't you going to the session?"

"Yes, I ought to be heading out that way soon. I suspect Seán won't be dropping by—he is probably heading out to the Dermott house now."

The words had only left his lips when they heard the front door opening. Kate turned around and saw the pudgy red face of Seán, evoking a labored breath from her that bordered on a groan.

"Jesus, it's like four seasons out there all in one day." He looked over at the snug. "Thought I would find you here, Gus. The misses won't be coming tonight—a touch of the stomach bug. Figured I would see if you wanted to walk out to the Dermotts' together."

As Kate listened, she was quick to decide that Seán's wife was probably fit as a fiddle, no doubt curled up in a robe, a glass of wine in one hand, and a good book in the other. She couldn't blame the woman for feigning illness to get a break from the half-wit she had been shackled to for more than a quarter of a century.

Thankfully, Seán was in a hurry to depart, so she didn't have the displeasure of his company for long. After the two men left, she resumed her duties for the night, checking things off her list between serving patrons. With many of the locals heading out to the Dermott house for the session, most of the clientele tonight were tourists. The pace was slow and easy, giving her far too much time to think about Finn and their meeting later on.

She took a quick peek out the window. The day started off quite beautiful, but now it looked as though someone had unfurled a bolt of gray fabric across the sky. Its drab color was compounded by the invasion of dark clouds, marching above like a well-organized brigade. They hung heavy, promising rain ahead, and she could only hope it would pour down and move on before her shift ended. There was no shelter from the elements out along the cliff walk, and the fierce wild Atlantic wind had already claimed a few of her umbrellas. She didn't plan to stay out long with Finn tonight, but she didn't want the weather to shorten their time together even more.

Just before midnight, she made her last call, though there were only a few patrons left in the pub. The rain was falling hard and steady, chasing away anyone who'd traveled in from town by foot.

Most of the inn's guests were nestled snug in their rooms for the night.

As the last couple filed out the door, she began her clean up. Knowing Finn would be waiting helped hasten her pace. As she worked through her closing routine, a dark shape caught the corner of her eye and she flinched, doing little to hide her surprise at the sight of Liam standing in the doorway. This was late for him to be moving out and about, being known to beat the sun to bed in the summer months.

His disheveled look hinted at interrupted sleep, and a flutter of excitement almost had her smiling. Had her parents arrived? The front desk staff were supposed to see them to their room when they turned up, but perhaps Liam wanted to let her know they were finally here.

"Kate," he started, but didn't go any further, his shoulders slumping.

She sized him up, noting his nervous look, which was odd for him. And she didn't miss that he'd balled his hands into fists, his knuckles white. A needling sensation gripped her gut. Had she done something wrong? Was Liam about to fire her? Was this about her greediness in taking that second cream puff? In hindsight, she had no regrets—that pastry was damn good.

He cleared his throat, the sound carrying to the shadowed corners. "There was an accident on the road from Shannon airport." His lips thinned, and a shudder ran across Kate's shoulders. "Your dad was driving the car."

"Dad is a terrible driver," she offered, holding the counter to steady herself. "Back home, he clipped a mailbox once downtown. They were picking up envelopes for a week. I can't say that I'm shocked he hit something. Does that mean they will be delayed?"

She watched as he bit hard into the inside of his cheek. Then her attention was caught by his clasped hands, his thumbs fidgeting.

"Kate, your mom and dad...won't be coming."

She raised her head to look him in the eye. "Like, not at all? They are okay, aren't they?" She blinked as tears welled.

"The accident was very bad, Kate."

The moon was barely visible through the gray clouds. Finn stood at the spot where he'd first happened upon her—that long-awaited moment in time that had occupied his every waking thought for years. With the light mist having grown heavier, his linen shirt was all but soaked through. Still, he waited. No amount of patience could compare to the century he had exhausted waiting for that fateful day when he first laid eyes upon Kate. He'd searched for her, never knowing the day the prophecy would come to fruition. All he could do was trust.

The fair-haired hero, the prince who had slayed all the dragons in the land, waited until the last minute of the night had passed and the sun greeted the day from the east. Soaked to the bone, he'd weathered the night but the promised princess never came.

Chapter Fifteen

For almost two months, Kate existed in an eternal fog. Her parents' funeral had taken place in a little country church a short distance away, and, thankfully, Liam and Edel saw to most of the arrangements. With no close relatives in Boston, she had agreed to have them buried here in County Clare. At the time, the journey back to the States was just more than she could endure.

Since then, her room became her refuge, and she hadn't bothered to leave even once. Like clockwork, her aunt brought breakfast, lunch, and dinner, clearing away the previous meal's dishes before she left. As she sat up in the bed, knees tucked tight to her chest, she felt as if she had slept more hours than humanly possible over the past few days. Even so, sleep did little to lift her spirits, not helped by her dreams being filled with guilt-ridden grief.

At twenty-four, it seemed unfair that she should have no parents. Her departure from Boston had been anything but amicable, their parting words still in her head with the mournful melody of a ship's foghorn. She'd never taken the chance to set things right, having waited too long, and now that opportunity was gone. The echoes of that failure were ever-present in her heart.

The compounding pain was unbearable. She wanted to tear at her hair and batter the walls like a lunatic locked away in an asylum. With all her might, she wanted to scream "No!" and demand that everything be unwound—brought back to the way it was before. Time was a savage mistress and death a heartless beast, but no amount of wanting could undo what was done. Even the salt of her tears failed to cleanse this gaping wound.

However, with almost two months having passed, and autumn well established, the haze of hurt thinned and she found herself wanting to reemerge into the world of the living again. She realized she had come to an emotional crossroads—a place where she could accept that she needed to heal, or fall deeper into the dark abyss. There would always be an emptiness in her—a hollow spot to remind her that she was alone in the world. She felt like an orphan, having no parents to calm her fears with a warm embrace. This was the reality that would remain a part of her forever, even if time dulled the edges of her pain.

She hated the way everyone tiptoed around her, but she had little energy to say so. Her fragility was so obvious that even Seán didn't dare make his usual jokes. By all accounts, she should have been pleased not to have to knock heads with him anymore. In truth, it made work boring. She had grown to enjoy their verbal sparring, relishing the challenge of remaining the clear victor in their battle of wits.

It had been such a long time since she'd seen Finn. While he'd probably understand why she stood him up that awful night, she would have preferred the chance to explain. She hadn't tried to see him and, to the best of her knowledge, he hadn't tried to see her either. If that were the case, why? He must have heard what happened? Word travels far and fast in rural Ireland. Anyway, since emerging from her room to resume some form of life, their paths had not crossed. If he wanted to see her, he would have made it happen, just as he had so many times before. He must have taken her failure to show as a rebuke—a final straw—and washed her from his memory altogether. She supposed their relationship was over, if it had even been anything at all.

It was a cool evening, even for late September, and she found it hard to believe that the summer had come and gone already. As she looked out the pub window at the rolling clouds hovering at the edge of Doolin, dime-sized raindrops fell, coating the ground and bringing that earthy sweet smell she'd come to know so well to the air.

She spotted Seán coming up the walk so tore herself from her comfortable perch, sure he would be soaked to the bone and drip all over the floor as usual. As she headed to grab a towel, he burst in through the doorway, nearly colliding with her and showering her with raindrops that had pooled on his trilby hat.

"What the devil?" he exclaimed. He caught his balance, giving her an apologetic nod. "Miss McCarthy, I didn't expect you there."

She smiled, shaking it off with a flick of her hand.

"Fine day out there," he said, tipping his hat and spilling the remaining water onto the floorboards.

"Fine day?" she snapped. "Why, it's as wet as an otter's pocket."

His eyes widened, his mouth falling open then closing, as if he wasn't sure if he should engage.

Kate pointed at the fresh puddle. "You made a mess on the floor. Who is going to clean it up?"

He looked down, his reflection glistening in the droplets by his feet. "So I did, Miss McCarthy. So I did." His voice had risen, shedding the muffled whisper he'd adopted around her these past two months. "I will take a pint, if you please. You can deliver it right over to me at the table by Old Gus."

With a loud thwack, he clomped across the floor in his wet boots, announcing to everyone in a one-block radius that Seán Campbell had arrived.

She pulled his pint, taking in the scene before her. Old Gus curled his weathered fingers around his tea cup and brought it to his lips for another sip. Out of sheer habit, he braced the delicate white saucer with his free hand, just in time for clumsy Seán to knock into the table as he dropped into the empty chair. Kate shook her head at the sight. Seán was anything but delicate.

"What's the story?" Old Gus asked, though he hardly needed to bother. If Seán had any news to share, he would do so without prompting. Now the man was seated, he replaced his cup upon the saucer.

"My cousin Joseph says there is bad business down in Limerick today."

"Oh, what does he say?" Old Gus asked, curling his hands along the edge of the table before hoisting himself forward.

"It's that new dual carriageway. Seems the fellow who did the planning failed to heed the whitethorn bush that sits along the route."

"A whitethorn? Well, that is bad business indeed." The seanchaí rubbed at his forehead as though he had a splitting headache.

"He told me the whole project is at a halt. Not a man on that crew will dare touch it."

Old Gus nodded. "Better to lose their jobs than to incur the wrath of the Good People."

"They will just have to change the path of that road." Seán sounded as sure about his proposed solution as he was his own name.

"I don't understand," Kate interjected, setting Seán's pint on the table. "They are going to put a halt to a major road project, all for a bush?"

The two men shot a look at her, and heat flushed into her face at the realization that she'd been caught eavesdropping. She took a few steps back and leaned against one of the empty tables.

"A whitethorn is not just any bush," Seán corrected, his look telling her she ought to know better. "That's a fairy bush," he whispered, then glanced around the bar to make sure no one had overheard the dreaded word.

"A lone bush," Old Gus added, drawing out each word.

"I don't understand what that means." Her ignorance on the matter made her feel foolish. In her defense, though, she'd heard so many of these stories that all the rules blurred together.

"A lone bush is very sacred to the Good People. They do not take kindly to those who dare to touch what is theirs. It would be like meddling with the graves in a churchyard. There are just some things you don't do. Mark my words, nothing but bad luck will befall those who are so unwise."

"I don't mean any disrespect," Kate said. "I just haven't heard of such a thing." She folded her arms and grimaced. "Every bush in the whole country belongs to the Good People? Don't you think that's a far reach? It all feels a bit too superstitious to me."

"You say we talk nonsense?" Seán responded, raising his hands in the air. "Didn't they string up a bunch of innocent women where you come from, all for a bunch of superstition? Seems things are not so different where you are from, Miss McCarthy."

"No, you're thinking of Salem, Massachusetts," she corrected, though she couldn't deny that he had a valid point. Even so, she wasn't about to admit it. To date, she had never seceded an argument, and she wasn't about to start now. "I come from Boston. It's about half an hour away, give or take."

Seán's mouth hung open, as if he couldn't believe she had countered with an argument so weak.

"So, Miss McCarthy, some guy says a curse is put on his cow and they go out and hang folks as witches? Sounds a bit like a superstitious place to me." His furry brows arched in a clear challenge to her.

"Yes, I admit America has its share of folklore and legends. That all happened in the late sixteen-hundreds, though, and some of it was more about greed and personal vendettas. Anyway, we have evolved considerably since then. Still, I admit there were many lives lost because of the belief that those men and women were witches. That's why I don't put stock in all of this hocus pocus here."

"They hung all those witches, but it appears they missed one," Seán said, giving Old Gus a wink.

"You are a vile little creature," Kate lashed back. "I can't help it if I don't believe in little winged creatures that will sprinkle me with magical dust. No, I can't honestly say I think any of that exists, any more than I thought any of those people in Salem were actually witches."

Old Gus gave her a sympathetic smile. "You have been ensnared by Victorian fiction, my dear. It's not your fault. It is little more than an image that has been entrenched in you from a young age. Tales of the old people are something entirely different. These are stories, regardless of how fanciful, seeded in truth, from the very people who witnessed their happening."

"You really think that, once upon a time, these people actually saw fairies?"

Seán winced at her use of the word, though she remembered he'd used it earlier.

"The Fae folk, or the Good People as I call them, are as real as you and I," Old Gus continued, his eyes showing his eagerness to share his knowledge. "They have been a part of this land since the dawn of time. In every victory and hardship, they have walked among the Irish people. You say the world has evolved, but the Good People stay eternally the same, bound to all the rules of their own kingdom."

"I guess what I struggle to understand is, if they are here, then why don't we see them? There seems to be so many people in the past who claim to have encountered the Good People. Where are they now?"

This was a question she had pondered since arriving in Doolin and hearing Old Gus go on about them. There was so much talk of the Good People, but always with stories that originated in the distant past. She could not help but wonder why there were so few stories from the present day.

"You're looking for those tiny winged creatures. The Good People can take many forms, but they can also look just like you and I. Do not be deceived by false notions."

"How do you know they are still out there?" she asked, determined not to give way. "Maybe we don't see them anymore because they just aren't there."

"Long ago, people were far more connected to the land. They had to walk everywhere they went. They covered long distances on foot. People would cross through fields, take a shortcut through the forests. Sightings were more common because people had to use the pathways that were available. If you want to find the Good People, you have to be where they are, outside in nature. Nowadays, people do less walking. They speed down main roads in their cars, barely noticing what's around them. Many shut themselves up in their houses, eyes glued to the television."

Kate couldn't argue with his logic. It made more sense than she cared to admit. People had become far too busy to appreciate the natural world anymore.

"We are so caught up in the flurry of our everyday lives," he continued. "We miss all the subtleties around us. A flicker of light, a shadow as it fades. There is a presence everywhere, in everything that we take for granted. We only see the surface, and yet there is so much hiding just beyond our sight. This is the place where the Good People dwell. They are the elemental, beings of nature, often in our own form. You cannot believe what you don't acknowledge, but they exist with or without our permission."

She sank into a chair, taking in all the seanchaí had said, aware that he was studying her as she scanned the length of the room, pausing at the shadows. If there was any truth to what he said, the Good People could be sitting among them now. Was it possible they passed her when she strolled down the streets of Doolin? Did she travel along their path when she used to walk the Cliffs of Moher at night? She always thought there was a powerful energy in Ireland, so unlike any other place she had been. It was a stretch of the imagination, but perhaps it was the energy of the Good People, both seen and unseen, going about their daily lives and co-existing with their human neighbors.

"You make a powerful argument, Gus. It is certainly something I need to think about." She may as well have waved the proverbial white flag.

"The world loves nothing better than a good mystery," he said, rubbing at his knees, his half smile telling her he was delighted that he'd managed to gain ground in their battle of wits. "It entices and entangles us. We gravitate to the excitement of something unknown, though the brain's natural wiring always desires an answer. It is the lingering possibilities that hold our interest."

Kate nodded, deciding to get a head start on drying and restocking the glasses before the crowd picked up.

"How is our host coming along with preparations for Friday night?" Gus asked as she got up, turning the focus back to Seán, who had by now managed to nurse his pint down to the last sip or two.

It was his week to host the session at his home. His excitement had been building, evidenced by his constant chatter over the past while. Kate struggled to hold back a smile as his eyes lit up like a child waiting for his birthday cake candles to be lit. He may have grated on her last nerve most days, but every now and then he showed an endearing side.

"Ready as ever. The wife is cooking up quite a spread." He slapped the table. "Miss McCarthy, will you join us this Friday evening, then?"

She looked back as she approached the bar. Caught off-guard, she stared at him for a few seconds. "Oh, I don't know..."

"I am starting to think that you don't like us. I might find myself personally offended if you should turn down my invitation, seeing as it is at my house and the wife has taken a great deal of trouble to get things prepared." He sipped the end of his pint, then shook his head as he faced Old Gus across the table.

"I-I probably shouldn't," she said, fumbling for the perfect excuse, but her mind drew a complete blank.

"What if you gave it a shot this once? It would not hurt you to have a bit of fun."

With the pressure bearing down on her, she responded with a subtle nod. "Maybe for a little while."

Seán clapped. "Now, that's the spirit."

Chapter Sixteen

On Friday evening, Kate wore her pale-yellow dress with little purple flowers on the skirt. For the first time since losing her parents, she sat at her dressing table and peered into the mirror. The dull lifelessness that had been a permanent fixture for months in her green eyes was gone. Never being one to spend a great deal of time on her appearance, today, as she dabbed a bit of blush on her freckled cheeks, she couldn't help but feel renewed. She fumbled around in her small drawer for the one tube of lipstick she owned—a faint shade of sheer pink. After dabbing it on, she smacked her lips together, taking in her reflection once more.

Her heart stung as a long-lost memory of her childhood came to her. She was seven years old, sitting at her mother's white wicker vanity table, layering on pounds of cold creams and blankets of lipstick. She closed her eyes to the image of her thin mother entering the room and gasping at the sight of her daughter coated in expensive cosmetics. Of course, she had been scolded for meddling with her mother's things but, at the time, she hadn't really cared. It was worth all the trouble for that moment of feeling so pretty.

After giving her hair a good brushing, she smoothed out her mass of curls into loose rippling waves, then leaned back, almost stunned at the woman staring back at her. She could not help but be pleased at what she saw. In truth, she didn't loathe getting dolled up quite as much as she let on, she just didn't like the vulnerability that came with such efforts. As with other women, she could become her own worst enemy if left to her own judgment. Her waistline was always too broad, her freckles too pronounced, her hair too unruly. It was far easier not to try because, when she dressed like other girls, she balked at comparing herself to them. She liked staying as far away from a level playing field as possible.

At least tonight, she had nothing to prove to anyone, happy not being in the market to woo any man with her looks. She didn't care if she was the least attractive woman at the Campbell house—the only thing she wanted was to suck up her pride and push all her worries aside. After months of darkness, she now wanted to hear music and laughter, and relish all the scents of the rich traditional Irish food wafting through the air. She wanted to hear stories of the Good People, the long-revered protectors of the land, and to spend the night surrounded by folk who lived life as it was intended—ones who never knew a day so gloomy that a ray of sunlight couldn't peek through the clouds. Tonight was about her emergence from the gloom, and there weren't any people better suited to show her the way than the Irish.

In the early evening, she set out on foot to Seán's humble farmhouse a mile or so outside the village. The crisp autumn air filled her lungs, renewing her spirit like a magical elixir. And the walk was just as healing, passing through the soft landscape of grassy fields, hanging on to the last shreds of green before the long cold nights of winter arrived. The cool air on her arms reminded her that she'd forgotten to bring a sweater, something she was sure to regret later. It was almost October, a time that would have been uncomfortably warm in Boston, but quite the opposite in the west of Ireland.

With welcome cheer, she swung the long umbrella she'd swiped from the pub, thankful to at least have remembered to bring it along. Even with the clear sky, this was a damp time of year, and you'd never know when an unexpected rain shower would come along. Though she'd been here for several months, adapting herself to the weather still proved difficult. Even so, she hadn't decided yet whether to stay in Doolin long-term or return to the States. Now her parents were gone, she had little reason to go back. The details of their estate were nearly settled, with all the logistics handled by the family's attorneys. Even if she was forced to return to deal with minor particulars, she doubted she would stay on. The thought of being back in Boston threatened her progress, laying raw the wound that was slowly starting to heal.

If she did choose to stay in Doolin, it might be a good idea to make some much-needed additions to her wardrobe. Though Liam and Edel seemed happy to keep her on at the inn, the tiny room she inhabited had become stifling. In time, she would need to seek out something of her own. The past months had left her feeling like a frightened child, scared of the great big world that loomed over her like a sleeping giant. She hated that vulnerability, having never been that person, even when her self-loathing was at its worst. What surprised her most was how much she wanted the old Kate back. The self-centered narcissist who, while pretending to know it all, still felt some shred of confidence in herself to overcome the most trying of circumstances. Despite her habit of berating herself for those imperfections, knowing her own character provided security. She wanted the woman she once was to return, scars and all.

A long gravel lane led off the main road to Seán's house, a well-kept two-story home with a steep pitched roof. The building was painted in a bright shade of yellow, reminding her of the thick coat of butter she had spread on her soda bread this morning. Its roof was tiled in gray slate, matching the two small barns off to the side. The property was bordered by a mix of weathered wood fencing and stacked stone walls, their bland hues brought to life by rows of purple forget-me-nots and dog violets.

She was relieved to see that she wasn't the first to arrive. A few cars were already lining the drive, and like herself, several people had come on foot. The front door stood wide open, and the sound of musicians tuning up their instruments in preparation for the night's session filtered out as she approached. Falling in step behind a young couple with a small child, she crossed the threshold, her nervousness weaseling its way into the pit of her stomach.

"Welcome, welcome," a petite-framed woman called out, emerging from the kitchen. She dusted her flour-covered hands off on her floral-patterned apron, then motioned for everyone to move further up the hallway and toward a back room.

Kate responded with an anxious smile.

"Why, bless my soul, it is Miss McCarthy. I swore on my prized hog that you wouldn't come tonight."

Seán's bellow startled her as he came down the stairs.

"You don't have any hogs," the woman said, moving to stand by his side as he descended the last step. "You only have sheep."

He flashed her a crooked smile. "Then I wouldn't have been out anything, had I lost."

By the woman's look of irritation, Kate could only assume that this was the unfortunate creature who had been married to Seán for more than thirty years.

"Sylvia Campbell," the woman said, reaching out.

Kate ignored the remaining flour on Sylvia's fingers and gave her hand a firm shake. "Kate McCarthy."

"Well," Seán said with glee, "let's show you the best Friday night you have had since you came to Ireland."

With an enthusiastic wave, he beckoned her to follow him down the hall to a large room. It was furnished with a mix of old hand-me-downs and a scattering of newer seating, with a line of mismatched chairs filling most of the empty spaces along the walls. She sat on one, tucked her handbag and umbrella underneath, and glanced around at all the other guests, relieved to see several familiar faces, a few of whom frequented the pub.

Not wanting to seem standoffish, she tried to think of some meaningless conversation to strike up as a growing number of people trickled in. On the cusp of launching, she was filled with relief when Old Gus shuffled through the doorway. In true fashion, he was greeted with the usual amount of acclaim, shaking hands with everyone who approached. It took a minute or two before he saw her, but when he did, his face lit up with delight.

"Miss McCarthy," he exclaimed. "What an absolute joy to see you here."

Taking up a chair beside her, he began an excited ramble about all the things she could expect from her first Friday session. She gave him her full attention, not bothering to remind him that she heard the same recounting every week at the pub. He was too deep in his element for her to steal away his thunder.

The night started with a heavy spread of foods, including Sylvia's famed cottage pie, a pot of coddle, and a plate of farls. Several other women had brought in cured salmon, seafood chowder, and a heaped dish of braised cabbage and bacon. All this was complemented by plates of cheeses and loaves of soda bread. Being polite, Kate took only small portions of each dish, but found herself wishing she didn't have such good manners. She could have heaped a good helping of everything onto her plate and not felt sorry. It was by far the best food she'd eaten since coming to Doolin, and she regretted not coming to the sessions before, though she doubted she would be able to fit into this dress if she'd done so. She always had a soft spot for good food, and an evening at the Campbell residence did not disappoint.

Music and dancing followed, and before long she found herself enveloped in the merriment. There was no room for sadness or worry in this place, and she laughed when Seán took his wife's hand to dance to a jig. When the musicians took a break, it was Old Gus's turn to take the floor. Settling in a wooden rocking chair by the fireplace, he waited as some of the children took their spot at his feet. The other guests scooted their chairs closer, everyone hoping to have the best view of the seanchaí.

"This one is a story from County Kerry," he began.

Kate couldn't help but notice how the old man's eyes twinkled as he spurred the imagination of all who listened.

"Along a lone road, in the darkest of hours, dwells the Leanan Sidhe, the fairy lover. A young man would do well not to travel by himself at night, for if she comes across you, she might decide that you are her next conquest. Those who she marks will be blessed with artistic enlightenment. The painter will create a masterpiece, and the musician will write a ballad that rivals the greatest of composers. Whatever talent you possess will be amplified by her power, so that everything you do can be matched by no other. Beware, though, the Leanan Sidhe will ask for much in return for these great gifts. Once a young man has come under her spell, he will remain so forever."

He shifted in his chair. "Perhaps it doesn't sound like a bad deal—after all, don't we all want fame and good fortune? Her affections are fleeting, however, and soon she will tire of you. No man who has ever won the love of the Leanan Sidhe lives a long life. For when she takes her next lover, the old one is turned to dust. So, mind you, young men, stay clear of traveling the roads after dark. Make your way home from the pub before the sun sets."

Kate gave a little chuckle, sure that this was another tale the wives had concocted to make sure their husbands made it home at a reasonable hour. But after working in the pub all summer, she was convinced it wasn't nearly as effective as they would have wished.

"Does this Leanan Sidhe have a sister named Sylvia?" Seán called out. "I think she has been trying to turn me to dust for thirty-some years."

"If she was my sister," Sylvia responded, "I'd be sure to find out a quicker way to get the job done, because my way is taking far too long."

A wave of laughter rippled through the crowd. Old Gus then continued with a longer tale he had heard in the southernmost part of County Clare. Even though Kate had gone back to working in the pub a few weeks after losing her parents, she struggled to recall much of anything she had done over that time. Her memories felt fuzzy and muted, and she realized now that she'd missed Old Gus's stories most of all. He probably shared one every night he visited the pub, but she hadn't been listening.

As he finished up his story, a tall man crossed the floor, giving Seán a pat between the shoulders.

"Seán, do you have some hazel rods I can come by and grab this week? My boy is planning on putting up a house on the back part of my land soon."

"I have a tree around the side," Seán replied. "I can get you some to plot it out."

"Hazel rods?" Kate repeated, curious.

Old Gus cleared his throat, and she flinched, having missed him returning to his seat beside her. He gave her a bright smile, ready to impart his wisdom, then rubbed at his knees, a habit he had when he was excited.

"You never build a house without first plotting it out with hazel rods. On each corner, you put two, and let them be for a day or two. If you return and they haven't been moved, then the building can proceed. If you come back and find they have been moved, then the house is smack dab in the middle of a fairy path."

"Is this like the lone bush thing? If you build on the path, you will incur the wrath of the Good People."

"Precisely," he said, delight spreading across his face. "I have known of a good many people who did not put stock in the old ways. Nothing good came of it. The Good People do not give up easily, especially when angered. If those rods are moved, his son had better change the layout of that house or move it entirely. It is that simple."

"What does it mean, though, to anger the Good People?" she asked, intrigued. "What harm could they really do?"

"A great deal of harm, if they so choose. A great deal of good, if they are inclined. I know you think these are just old stories, passed down from superstitious folks, but I assure you as sure as I live that I have known both the blessings and the wrath of the Good People. I have seen men put to ruin when they failed to heed the warnings. There was a time when the death of a couple of good horses or livestock could send a family into utter ruin. You may think times are different now, but that's not the case. The wrath of the fairies is nothing to trifle with, my dear. Seán knows this as well as I, he is just not so eloquent with his manners."

"That's a bit of an understatement," she said with a haughty laugh. "I guess I'm just torn. On one hand, I can honestly say there are things that defy my imagination, but some of these stories are just a bit of a stretch."

"Give it time. This is the most mystical place on earth. All you have to do is pay attention to what is around you. In time, you will have all the proof you need."

She released a deep sigh. Old Gus was an accomplished storyteller, but something in her stopped her believing he was intentionally lying to her. The seanchaí was anything but a liar. He believed what he said wholeheartedly. And she couldn't dispute that Ireland held its own kind of magic. There was always something hovering at the edges of one's senses. She knew what he meant by needing to pay attention, though she doubted her mind was ever quiet enough to really see much of anything.

Her dad loved a good ghost story, and held true to an old family tradition stemming back from Victorian times of telling scary tales at Christmas. Every Christmas Eve, they would sit by the light of the family tree as he recounted some old stories he'd heard as a child. Some of these scared the wits out of her, and she would stay awake all night, not sure if it was in anticipation of Santa, or for fear she might look up and find some gray shadow crossing the room. She remembered her father saying that the innocent minds of children gave them the ability to see what adults could not detect.

She pondered Old Gus's words. Once upon a time life had been simple, though not easy by any stretch of the imagination. Was the unending grind of life responsible for severing a person's ability to connect to the land?

The night sped by so fast, she didn't notice how late it was until she realized the sun had set, with only the charcoal-gray sky visible through the windows at the side of the room. She'd stayed far longer than planned, but was happy to have attended. It was the best she had felt in a long time.

She got up, grabbed her umbrella and threw the strap of her bag over her shoulder, then crossed the room to where Old Gus was chatting with one of the musicians. After bidding him farewell, she promised to share how she felt about attending her first session when he visited the pub tomorrow. On her way out, she stumbled upon Sylvia and thanked her for her warm hospitality.

After a few more parting good-byes, she headed down the hall to the front door.

"You can't go out there alone," Seán called out just as she reached for the handle. He scurried down the hall, his breathing ragged. "It's best you wait till the rest of the group starts back into the village."

"I've already stayed far longer than I intended." She tapped the glass face of her watch. "I have to work in the morning."

"It's dark out."

She blinked at him, wondering why he'd think that fact wasn't obvious to her.

"The Good People will be moving about at this hour. They travel from place to place under the cover of darkness." He wiped his chin with the back of his hand. "It's best if you go back with the group."

His tone was more persistent than before, and she gave a half-hearted grin, her heart warmed. Normally, she and Seán took great joy in being at odds with each other, but even if she thought he was talking nonsense, he seemed to have a genuine concern for her well-being.

"I will go straight home," she said, patting her hand across her heart like she was swearing an oath. "It's not far."

He kicked the toe of his boot against the wood floor. Just when he looked to be teetering on relenting, he held his forefinger up, as if having conjured the most splendid idea.

"Take this with you," he said, hiking up his pant leg. He fumbled around inside the top of his boot before drawing out a tiny leather sheath. Next, he unclipped a button on the strap and pulled a small black-handled knife halfway out. Kate looked down at it in bewilderment, then back at Seán, who flashed a gleaming smile back at her. "The Good People will not bother you as long as you carry a black-handled knife with you."

He snapped the button shut and pushed the sheath into her hand. Old Gus had mentioned the Good People's avoidance of knives such as this but she'd never considered carrying one around.

The persistence in Seán's eyes left her with little hope he would let the matter rest.

"What about you? What will you do for protection until I get this back to you?" She curled her fingers around the object.

"Don't worry about me." He flicked his hands as if shooing away a fly. "I can get it back from you next time I'm in the pub. Besides, I have its twin in my other boot."

Too tired to put up an honest fight, and touched by his gesture, she responded with a quick nod, then tucked the knife into her handbag.

"Thank you again for the invitation, and your hospitality. I am really glad I came. I had a lovely time."

"We Irish know a thing or two about hospitality," he said, his eyes bright. "I hope to see you at next week's session, Miss Mc-Carthy. It is good to see you getting out and about."

"Maybe," she replied. "I really needed this more than I thought."

Seán turned and headed back toward the house party, still in full swing. She waited until he was out of view, then retrieved the knife and set it on the hall table before opening the door and stepping out into the night air.

Chapter Seventeen

Doonagore House wasn't far, maybe a twenty-minute walk on a clear day. Had she realized she would leave the session so late, she may have opted to take her scooter. Walking, though, was the only way to fully appreciate the hidden beauty of Doolin and its environs, even at night.

At the edge of the village, she walked into a mist, which wasn't an unusual occurrence so close to the cliffs. However, it wasn't long before it grew heavier and engulfed her, making it impossible to see her own hand. She stopped and looked back in the direction of Seán's house, thinking it might have been wiser to wait for the group after all. But Liam needed her to help out at the front desk in the morning, and she loathed those early hours already so was eager to make it home and try to get some sleep. It wasn't too far. She just needed to be careful where she walked.

As she continued on, all she had to guide her way was the sound of her steps on the side of the road. Even as she tried her best to move in a straight line, her sense of disorientation was palpable, and she jumped when wet grass brushed against her ankle as she veered off her intended course. The road was so narrow, two cars could barely pass in the best of conditions, and that wasn't lost on her as she moved along. Her spine stiffened as she strained to listen for approaching vehicles. As much as she wanted to quicken her pace, it was impossible, with the fog leaving her far too vulnerable to try. Even the dark sky was unseen, as was the faithful light of the moon, shrouded by the foggy veil. All around her was bleak grayness, and she cursed herself for daring such a foolish venture.

Then the somewhat comforting rhythm of her own footsteps was broken by a sound behind her. It was faint at first, and she hastened her pace, going against any common sense she had left. The old seanchaí had spoken of nights like this, and the dangers that awaited a lone traveler on a desolate road. She tried her hardest to remember what he'd said. Was it along the roads of County Clare or the Ring of Kerry? She was damned if she could remember, for she'd heard so many stories, they all blurred together. The sound grew louder, and brought up the memory of the dark tale of the Leanan Sidhe—the fairy lover. She sighed with relief on recalling that the Leanan Sidhe was known to concentrate her efforts on young men who traveled the roads late at night and, in that moment, she was never more grateful to have been born a woman, but that did little to ease her disquiet at the prospect that someone was following her, and drawing closer. Even if she wasn't likely prey for the Leanan Sidhe, it didn't stop her thinking of all the other possibilities. She upped her pace, her focus fixed on what she hoped was the road ahead, but when she glimpsed a dark presence in the corner of her eye, she stopped dead in her tracks, turning left and right as she tried to decide what to do.

Everything around her fell silent, save for her heavy breathing and her heartbeat thundering in her ears.

Then fingers grasped hold of her bare arms, and she leapt and screamed at the same time.

"It's me," a man whispered, releasing her. "It's just me."

"F-Finn?" What the hell? She held both hands over her heart, fearing it would explode. It had been so long, yet his voice was as familiar as the softness of her favorite pillow. Her thoughts were as scrambled as her stomach, and nameless rage filled her bones. She flailed her umbrella out around her like a sword, making contact with what she assumed was his head.

"Ouch!"

"You bloody bastard! You scared the hell out of me."

"On the contrary, you blasted woman," he snapped back. "All the evil spirits are alive and well in you."

She growled deep within herself, scrunching her face up, though it mattered little—he couldn't see her face anyway.

"Why the hell didn't you say something? It's common courtesy to make your presence known, especially on a night like this."

"I wasn't sure it was you at first," he reasoned. "I had to be sure."

"So, you just go out on foggy roads and grab strangers? What if it wasn't me? What then?"

"I would have just disappeared back into the shadows, like I always do." His chuckle pierced the fog, and she glared out at the smug grin she was sure would be scrawled upon his face.

"You can't be out here on your own. It isn't safe." He said it like an overbearing dad. One she no longer had.

"It's just a bit of fog," she replied, knowing it made her sound all the more foolish. She had grown up on the New England coast and was no stranger to a foggy night, but this surpassed anything she had ever seen in Boston.

"I wasn't talking about the fog."

"I was doing just fine. The walk home is not that far."

She flinched when he touched her arms again, but didn't step away.

"You're trembling?"

"I forgot my sweater," she spat, stepping away this time. "And there's a breeze."

"The air is pretty still. I don't feel a breeze at all."

"Are you just going to stand here and argue about the weather? Can we get moving already?"

"Yes. I think that would be best. After all, it is getting late."

He looped an arm under hers and guided her in the direction of the inn, or at least she hoped so. The warmth of his bare skin on hers was calming, and it wasn't long before she felt herself relaxing. However, her sense of safety with Finn by her side was little more than a comfortable illusion. In reality, there were now two people in grave peril, and that had a knot of guilt twisting in her stomach.

Her foolish desire to travel out here alone had put Finn in danger too.

"Why did you come out here after me? Aren't you afraid that the Leanan Sidhe will come and take you away as her lover?"

"Not the road she travels," he stated. "Besides, she wouldn't bother the likes of me."

"Don't be so sure of yourself. Perhaps she takes a shine to prattish jerks who accost women in the dark. You might get a dose of your own medicine, for once."

"Nah, she wouldn't bother her own kind."

His comment registered but she was unsure what he meant and, deciding further debate was unwinnable, she ceased talking. They walked along in silence, Finn guiding her into the ever-blind space ahead. After a few minutes, he stopped, maintaining contact with her arm.

"Enough of this," he said, his words carrying on a low grumble of frustration.

He blew out a long heavy breath, as though he'd held it in his lungs for days. Kate blinked several times, astounded as the fog began to part, like the waters of the red sea.

"What just happened?" she demanded, seeing his face clearly for the first time.

"Nothing." He shrugged, urging her on again. "The fog just cleared. That's all."

She picked up her pace, pulling her arm from his. "Something just happened. You blew out a deep breath and something just happened."

He gave her a side-eye glance. "Don't be preposterous."

She bristled at his rebuke. I know what I saw. At least I think I do. Her confusion was replaced by a deep-held mix of anger and disappointment that had lurked within her over the last two months, and the sheer power of its sudden manifestation left her on the verge of exploding. Considering Finn was the only person close to hand, and given the absurd circumstances, there was nowhere else it could be released toward.

"Why are you even here? I haven't seen you in two months. When I might have needed a friend, you were a ghost. I do not need you now."

She stared at him, expecting some profound response, and maybe a reminder of how it had been she who stood him up that night. He may not have known the reason why, but she was in no mood to take the blame. She'd allowed herself to believe that there was some dazzling spark between them but, when push came to shove, Finn was like everyone else in her life—quick to forget her when the going got rough.

He opened his mouth, as if to say something, but closed it again. And all the lonesomeness in his eyes did nothing to sway her.

"I don't want this," she said, waving her free hand around the narrow space between them. "I don't want you. I don't want castles and buttercups or black-handled knives. I don't want fairytales and heartache. I don't want the freedom that comes from dead parents. All I want is Kate." She pounded her breastbone. "Just me. Not an ounce of help from anyone. Just me."

Even in the darkness of the pale moonlight, his eyes looked like shattered glass. She averted her gaze to cut off potential remorse for her words.

"All I want is what you want, Kate. All I want is Kate."

His words hung heavy around her, making her think that, had the situation been different, they would have stripped the air clean out of her lungs. While she had reason to be angry at Finn, most of the venom in her words was reserved for her life as a whole.

"Did you know about my parents?" she asked, hell bent on inflicting as much pain on herself as on him.

"Yes," he whispered, looking at the ground.

His growing discomfort only fueled her senseless rage. She had never been one to deny her own stubbornness, but never stooped so low as outright cruelty. It was as if something in her snapped. She wanted someone, anyone, to hurt the same as her. And even though she knew she'd regret her words tomorrow, it didn't stop her.

"If you care so much about me, why didn't you try to see me?"

"You didn't leave your room for so long. By the time you did, I thought it might be too late. I expected, after all that had happened, you just didn't want to see me anymore." He took a step closer, as if to reach out, but she stepped back, knowing too well how her defenses diminished at his touch.

"And you couldn't so much as put a note under my door?" Desperate to stay in control, she knew she was grasping at anything to keep the argument going.

"No."

"Why not?" she snapped.

"The iron handle on your door."

She glared daggers at him, but then, like the parting of the fog, something changed and she closed her eyes, steeling herself as echoes of the not-so-distant past flooded in with such ferocity, she found herself stumbling backwards. The air felt cooler, perhaps even thinner, her lungs filling with its lightness.

Her vision was hazed by the near-veiled image of Old Gus rubbing at his knees, excited, the hint of pine in his cologne filling her senses as he leaned in to share some delicious secret:

"They won't go near iron. A black-handled knife is a good deterrent. Running water is another of their weaknesses. Remember when I told you about Spectacle Bridge? Now you know why."

She swayed back and forth, lulling herself in the midst of her memories. Finn didn't reach out to steady her as he had before. Maybe he was standing still, like a stone monument waiting for the curious passersby to read its placard, wanting her to see something he'd hidden away for far too long. Something that lay right before her this entire time.

Hindsight pummeled her with all its force, knocking off her rose-tinted glasses and shattering them into specks. When she opened her eyes, she saw Finn as never before. She saw everything.

He was beautiful, carved from the dust of stars to shine just as brilliantly. There wasn't an ounce of his flesh that wasn't unflawed, with every inch of him designed to such perfection she could almost feel the salty sting of her tears as they pooled. Even in the depth of darkness, gold gleamed as it danced through his hair, and those gray eyes, drenched in some nameless pain, yet as pure as a morning with no breeze. His tall frame was bound together by sinew and muscle, sculpted by the master artisan of the gods. He was exquisite, and for a blip in time he had been hers, some faraway dream she'd plunged headfirst into, never so much as bothering to interpret its meaning.

She didn't need to see him move closer to know he had. He was so near, his heat almost seared her skin, and as they shared the same breath, his scent was like the night air dripping with the sweet smell of turf, leather, and salty sweat. The energy around them was like the space in time between the strike of lightning and the first growl of thunder.

Her mind traveled back to the slow burn of his silky lips on her own, sending tiny shocks to the deepest roots of her hair. She was unequivocally and undeniably in love with him, but when she had hurled herself from that cliff, she could not recall. All she knew was that the freefall had been glorious, but too good to ever feel again, even for a dreamer like her.

She had allowed herself to get drunk on the idea that, for once, she might be good enough, and that somewhere out there someone existed who didn't need her to change. Of the millions of people on this earth, she had somehow managed to stumble upon the one meant for her—the man who could bring love and light back into a life spent hunkering in the shadows. That was the way of it, wasn't it? Every single sign had been right there in front of her, from the way he looked at her the first night they met, to how he took her in now. Finn had only been hers because he was not…real. Even if her heart was in staunch disagreement, none of this was real.

He told her one time that love doesn't cause pain, and he'd been right. Love had not brought this pain, only the loss. It was that hollow place where the heart calls out into the empty void, wishing back what once had been. She wanted the comfortable illusion to return, but that was long gone now. Now she knew he wasn't real, the question of what he was remained.

"I think you are a villain, Finn. I think that ever since the day we met, you have replaced all the dark clouds in my life with even darker ones. Just what harm do you intend to bring me?" She eyed him, studying every aspect of his features, even the texture of his skin. He may have felt so true, but he wasn't carved of the same flesh and blood as her.

"I have never meant a moment's harm to you, but I have brought it just the same."

His eyes held all the sadness of the world, and she realized that the strength she had manufactured was fading. It would be so easy to reach out and give him some comfort, lessening the guilt she felt for berating the man. She didn't, though, because she couldn't give any more of her heart to someone she was sure had deceived it.

"Who are you? What are you, Finn?" Her voice was coarse and unyielding.

His left cheek lifted in a half-grimace. "You have rules in your world, and I have rules in my own. I'm caught somewhere in the in-between."

"Stop speaking in riddles," she snapped, in no mood to read between the lines. "Tell me, right now."

He stepped back and sat on the flat edge of a stone wall that bordered a curve in the road. Kate glanced down the desolate road, then over to where he sat, wondering whether she should just stay put. At this point, getting smashed by an oncoming lorry didn't seem like such a bad way to end the night. However, common sense gnawed at her and she decided that it wouldn't be fair to the lorry driver to have to peel her off his windshield. She moved to the roadside, disregarding Finn's subtle pat on the spot beside him. It was pointless, considering it was just the two of them out here on this empty stretch, but something in her needed to keep a safe distance.

"It was eighteen forty-five, the first year of the great blight," he began, his tone solemn. "I lived a happy life among my people. The Good People, as you would know them. One day, a curse was put upon an old hawthorn tree by an angry man spitting his rage against the land. As I say, rules in my world are not like your own. When a curse is put upon our home, one must be chosen to answer for it." He looked up to his left, as if recalling that fateful day in full color.

"It was you?" she said, her impatience getting the better of her. "You were the one chosen."

"No matter how hard I tried, he would not let me go. So, in return, I brought him every kind of misfortune. I was relentless in my spite, but no evil deed could compare to what he was already enduring. Starvation had taken his son, and his daughter was close to death. Something in my heart softened as I watched her clinging so close to her end. I wanted to atone for the needless harm I had brought this man. He was suffering so much, and this blackness in my heart was taking its toll. I wanted to make it right, but that night as I wandered the fields, I came upon the banshee. I knew then, it was too late."

Kate went cold at the mention of the banshee. The stories had built up so strong in her mind, she hardly thought of them as folklore anymore.

"She died, then?" she choked out, thoughts of her own parents still so raw. "The girl?" How could this place, so etched in beauty, cloak so much darkness?

"They both did. She of starvation and he of a broken heart. With his last words, he released me from the curse. He had kindness in his heart for me, even when I did nothing but seek my revenge on him. This was such a cruel world, and since I was released, I wanted to return home to my world among my own people. But I knew I couldn't. I had done so much wrong in this place that my mind would never be free of that haunting memory." He clawed at the palm of his hand, as if trying to scratch away some haunting sin.

As she regarded him, she couldn't help weigh the similarities between them both. Just as she was alive, so was he, but in his own time and space. By some shift in nature, some bend in the heavens, their two worlds crashed into one another on a pale moonlit night against the infinite horizon of a turbulent sea. Two lost creatures, outrunning poor decisions and fending off the past.

"You didn't go back home, even though you had the chance." She thought back to her mom and dad, knowing they would have wanted her to return home. It was probably the sole purpose of their visit. For them, cooler heads had prevailed, but she had no intention of being compliant. She had planned on rejecting a return to Boston, if only to spite them.

"I had to face my justice. I would have never been happy until I paid for my wrongdoings. I honestly didn't know what to do. I started to roam, crisscrossing the country, searching for anything that would bring me peace, and finding absolutely nothing. Then, one day, I came upon a woman. A very special woman."

"A suitor?" She almost apologized, aware that her snarky, ill-placed attempt at humor was a selfish effort to break the tension.

Finn's face remained as smooth as burnished stone, undaunted by her response. His story had become far too relatable, and she teetered on reacting with empathy. Yet another emotion she could not afford if she was to stay mad, and she needed to remain angry.

"I was traveling along one of our routes. A road for the Good People—a fairy road, they call it. I heard a faint crying. It was such a mournful sound, one that made you think someone had harvested all the sadness in the world and burdened it upon one heart. I approached her slowly, confident she could not see me unless I wanted her to. She was tending to a little herb garden outside her cottage. You couldn't believe my shock when she turned, wiping away stray tears and looking right at me."

"She could see you, even though you didn't want her to?" She took a step forward, her curiosity holding her in a stranglehold.

"Biddy was gifted with the sight, you see," he said, his eyes sparkling in the darkness.

Kate's breath caught. "Wait! Biddy Early? The Biddy Early from Feakle? The bean-feasa?"

"You know of Biddy," he said, reminding her of that night long ago when she'd shared Old Gus's warning.

"I think everyone does. She is a County Clare legend." She stepped forward again and touched the edge of the wall, staying an arm's length away as she sat on it.

"She was a powerful woman. No one knew the art of healing better than she, but like me she found herself caught between the two worlds. Biddy could interact with the world of the Fae, just as I could that of humans. I felt connected to her sadness—drawn to it. You see, Biddy had lost her one and only son, and no amount of time could stifle her unending grief at the loss of him. Despite all the good our own powers could accomplish, neither of us were able to do the thing we wanted most, to save others. So connected, we were, that we vowed to help each other."

Kate realized she was leaning forward, eager to know more. After a few seconds, though, she snapped straight. "Are you going to finish this story? For crying out loud, do not leave me hanging."

"Biddy could see a great many things, but she wanted to see her son most of all. Life was anything but easy for her in those days. She was well-known in these parts, but her work had not managed to bring her wealth. I wanted to help her to be able to see the son she so desperately missed, and give her something that might also help her financial woes. When I gave her the blue bottle, I knew it would bring her good fortune for the rest of her days."

"The blue bottle? Biddy really did have a bottle that would let her see the future?" She shook her head in disbelief, wondering if she would have the courage to relay such a story to Old Gus, doubting she could sound as convincing as Finn. How would the seanchaí react? She had scoffed so many times at such tales, he might think she was poking fun.

"Biddy could see the past and the future, actually," Finn continued. "She already had the sight, and the bottle just gave her the whole picture. She could see the cause and effect of everything."

The dots joined in Kate's head. "That's why she was so reputed for her skills. The advice she gave was because she could see how any given situation started and how it might end. Now I understand Old Gus's comment—if Biddy said to do something, you had to follow it to the letter." She leaned forward. "Tell me, did she get to see her son?"

"Of course," he replied, his voice edged with emotion. "It was the least I could do for her, given all she managed to do for me."

Kate clasped her hand over her mouth. In all this talk of Biddy and her blue bottle, she had forgotten that this miraculous woman must have returned Finn's kindness in some way. She inched forward and nudged his arm. "Go on, tell me more."

"Biddy had a way of peering into the depths of your soul. With the bottle, she saw the bleakness of my past. She passed no judgment whatsoever, though—'twas not in her nature. She was the most giving being I had ever met, and that day she gave me real hope—something I held onto every day until the night the prophecy came true. That was the night I met you, Kate."

She leaned back, her mouth hanging open. "I'm sorry, I was part of Biddy Early's prophecy more than a hundred years ago? Forgive me, Finn, but you have lost me now."

"Biddy had many attributes, with knowledge of every herb and plant, and could cure anything with one of her remedies. She knew the ways of the Good People, what brought their blessing and what incurred their wrath. It was a given that I must face retribution for what I had done. She had boundless intelligence and a fiery spirit to match." He smiled as he looked into the distance. "I can still remember how the flush of her cheeks matched her flaming red hair. She became a very dear friend to me, until the day she died."

Kate pursed her lips and folded her arms. "Are you sure Biddy didn't have designs on you herself?"

"For a time, I thought I might be in love with her, but she never returned my affections. She told me that I would wander for many years. Then, one day, when I least expected it, I would come across a woman and stare into the face of Biddy herself, with red hair that lit up the night like a flaming candle, and green eyes that sparkled like flawless emeralds."

As far as she knew, no pictures of Biddy existed, but she had difficulty believing that she and the famed seer of Clare were dead ringers for each other.

"That wasn't everything. And please stop interrupting me."

"Huh?" She gawked at him, his deep frown conveying his irritation. She hadn't said a word, this time, but knew she was guilty as charged. Interrupting was one of her countless bad habits. "Go on, then."

"Biddy said this woman would play a song that set my soul on fire. That I would know it was her in the spot where all the buttercups bloomed. It's just as Biddy said it would be. You are the one, Kate. There can be no doubt."

She touched her bottom lip. "The buttercups. Biddy really said all these things?"

"Biddy did have a warning, though." He brushed something she couldn't see off his knee. "Fate had not allowed all the blackness in my heart to be at rest. It was still out there waiting, and would plague my own happiness as I had the farmer's. She told me I would not win the girl's heart so easily. That I would be faced with a decision not to be taken lightly. If I made the right call, things would work out as they should. In the end, the one I was destined to love had to choose me in return. She left me no more than that. I don't know how her vision ends. I only know that, when she died, the blue bottle disappeared."

Again, he stared off into the distance. Kate thought back to the night at Cahermann Hill, and how she had seen something in his mood change as he looked into the darkness. Had he sensed something? Had he known? With her no longer lost in the story of Biddy, the hollowness of her loss crept to the fringes of her heart, and her neck and shoulders went cold when it came to her.

"My parents? Did you know what was to happen to them?"

"No," he said. "Not exactly."

"What do you mean by 'not exactly'?" She gripped her umbrella, tempted to give him another whack. "Did you know they were going to die? It is a pretty straightforward question, Finn. I want an answer."

"When I got to the bridge, she was there waiting for you."

She blinked a rapid sequence as she took herself back. Finn hadn't gone with her to the bridge. A chill rippled through her bones.

"Who?"

"The banshee," he answered, his voice low, as if uttering the word might bring her out of the mist. "She had set her sights on you. You were never supposed to cross that bridge."

Kate sat frozen, his voice echoing in her head, as if from a distance, cutting through the manifesting images. The comb. The one on the floor of the pub that day. It was meant for her. The banshee, this creature she had so casually dismissed as a superstitious myth, was real after all.

"But I did make it over the bridge," she whispered. "Why didn't she take me when she had the chance? Why my...parents?"

"She is a bean-feasa of great power. Still, she doesn't take lives, only foretells of what is to come. If it is death, then that cannot be changed, but at times she can shift the winds, and her prediction can fall upon another. I bartered with her." Even in the dark, she saw his Adam's apple bobbling as he swallowed. "I pleaded for your life, Kate."

Her temples throbbed. "You saved my life, but you sacrificed my parents in my place?"

"I offered her two souls in return for yours, but I never knew who they would be. Yes, I knew they would be connected to you in some way, and you would not escape the grief of their loss. The only thing I could be sure of was that it would not be you, and so I made the deal."

"The second comb," she muttered.

His brows furrowed as he looked at her. She had never mentioned the second comb, thinking it a practical joke. Right then, her heart was being torn in every direction. Regret, unlike mistakes, could never be outrun. This would stay with her for all time. Her parents, who spent their lives giving everything they had to their maelstrom of a daughter, gave the last thing they could, for the final time. It was her fault they were gone. She had become the monster she always thought she was—the bringer of storm clouds, and no summer day was safe in her wake.

As much as she wanted to take her fury out on Finn, she couldn't find the strength. He had bartered for her life with the banshee, not knowing for sure how the debt would be paid. While he'd saved her life, he could not save her from the cost. Looking at him, his heart laid out, ready for her to trample, she felt nothing but pity. What he intended as a good deed altered both their lives in the end. Neither he nor she would be free from knowing the pain they had caused others. Now they were just two people, doomed to live in the shadow of ghosts. Ghosts of people. Ghosts of their own regrets. Now, they were both alone, but for each other.

She took his hand in hers. "You could not have known what was to come. It isn't your fault."

"I have caused you the greatest pain, but it was never what I intended. All that darkness was meant for me. It was supposed to be my debt to pay. You have to know that I only made the deal to save you. I honestly did not weigh the consequences. I can't lie to you. I cannot say I would have done differently if given the choice. I just never wanted things to end this way."

"I know I should be grateful for what you did to save my life," she said, stifling an emotional surge she couldn't afford to release. "I have spent my entire life ignoring every red flag set before me, but I can't be that person anymore. It is time I grew up and saw the world for all that it is, a merciless place. For a moment, I thought I could feel myself falling in love with you, but that girlish notion has flown away with everything else that mattered in my life. We created this place where it's us against the world, but the cold hard truth is that the world is still here. It's sitting right between us, providing all the reasons why you and I can never be together."

"Can't we just write it out of our fairytale?" he asked, his eyes pleading. "We can still have our castle, just you and I."

"Even Biddy knew it would never be that simple," she said, her heart aching with every word. "This isn't love, Finn. We barely know each other. Feelings are not facts. We just like the idea of love, but it isn't real." She released his hand. "I don't think I am the one you have been searching for all this time. I think she is still out there."

He shook his head. "I have more reasons to love you than I don't. Can't you see that the universe has aligned to bring us together? There is such a thing as fate. You were meant to come here, just as I was meant to find you. My soul is entwined with yours—I cannot be set free."

"I am not holding you here. You are as free now as the day we first met. I am not yours and you are not mine. It really is that simple."

Her stomach clenched at the callousness in her voice. She cared for him so much more than this bitterness in her heart would allow. As much as it pained her to be so cruel, she couldn't afford to give him hope that wasn't there, that she wasn't going to fulfill. In time, she would break his heart—it was the only thing she knew how to do in relationships. Better now than later, when she found herself in too deep to leave him anymore unscathed than she was now.

"I can respect that you feel that way, Kate, but it is not so simple for me. I have spent so many years searching for you, I cannot just walk away. Wherever you go, whatever you do, there won't be a day when your voice doesn't call to me. You are like warmth in the bleak cold of winter."

"You, Finn, are my winter. Truth be told, I despise that season most of all."

With those last words, she got to her feet and walked away. If Finn followed, she didn't know or care—she wasn't going to turn around. This nightmare disguised as a dream was at an end.

Chapter Eighteen

"I am in love with him, Old Gus," she said, all too aware of the lack of joy in her words. "But I think you know that my suitor is not just any suitor. I think you know far more than you let on."

The seanchaí gave a wry grin, as though happy that, at last, she had figured out what he'd known for a while. Had he not been such a kind soul, she might have pelted him for failing to tell her. It was her life after all. But the storyteller was ever perceptive. Try as she might to deny her feelings about Finn, Old Gus had always seen straight through her thinly veiled objections.

"I think Biddy would know what to do," he said, nodding to himself. "She was a wise woman. A very good woman."

"How can Biddy help me? She has been gone for nearly a hundred years." She rolled her eyes in frustration. While she loved County Clare—she really did—she longed for the day when her life would be straightforward and simple. Everything here was so cryptic, with nothing spelled out. The constant need to decipher each detail had her feeling weary.

"Miss McCarthy, the world has gone and got itself into a big hurry. No one believes in the old ways anymore. They think they are too old fashioned. No one believes in magic, but I am here to inform you these are not just stories I tell. I have seen magic with my own eyes, and now you have too."

"I am tired of magic, Gus. I am tired of feeling like I am shoulders-deep in some Sherlock Holmes' mystery every waking minute of the day. I want to go back to the days when my life was normal and boring. I know every girl wants this dream romance—a perfect duet with some dashing handsome prince in an ivory-towered castle. Right now, I just want a guy who is one-hundred percent, without a shadow of a doubt, human. Is it too much to ask that, when I finally find the right guy, he might actually be from my own world?"

"Long distance relationships can be tough," Old Gus said, his left eye squinting above a crooked smile. "I suppose living in two different worlds would have its own set of challenges."

"Forgive me if I don't acknowledge your attempt at humor, but this is serious. What am I to do?"

He lifted his right hand off his lap, palm out, in a clear gesture for her to calm herself. "Just on the outskirts of Feakle, there is a small country road, rarely traveled. If you follow the stone wall that lines the field, you will come across an old metal gate. Just across the road lies a narrow pathway. It's quite overgrown, and most people wouldn't give it a second glance but, if followed, it will lead you right to Biddy's old cottage."

Kate's jaw went slack, and for a moment the words wouldn't come. She had forgotten that Biddy's house still stood, or the frame of it at least. It shouldn't have surprised her, because most of the houses around Doolin were as old. She just hadn't considered that the place where this famed woman once lived would be relatively close.

"Biddy's cottage," she murmured, her hands tingling with the excitement surging through her.

"It is not a place for you to go out traipsing around by yourself," Old Gus said, his voice firm. "If you are so inclined to go, I would be more than willing to take you." He leaned forward. "If you have any shadow of doubt about the magic that exists in this land, a trip to Biddy's will cure you. I must give you a stern warning, though. Nothing, and I do mean nothing, can be disturbed there. It is as protected by the Good People today as it was in Biddy's time. Do not take a single thing that is not of the earth. You have seen the power they possess. Do not test it further,"

An icy sensation frittered through her. After what happened to her parents, she could hardly bring herself to call them the Good People anymore. The frightening reality of the beautiful and dangerous world that circled her, unseen, was almost too much to fathom, its balance so delicate. A house built in an unsuitable spot, a berry plucked from the wrong bush, something as simple as crossing over a bridge at the incorrect hour—anything could infuriate these invisible beasts.

Even if there was more to Finn than she had once thought, it was still difficult to come to grips with. If there was any truth to his story, then, in all this time, he had never been honest. More than once, she'd laid bare her deepest regrets to him, and he'd held back from telling her anything. It wasn't as if this was an inconsequential matter, like failing to tell her that he had a library book overdue, or those golden locks were not his natural color. Failing to mention that he was part of what she once thought was a mythical race of beings, was sort of a big deal, at least to her. How could she even begin to trust him?

Chapter Nineteen

Just after sunrise on Friday morning, Kate stepped out into the growing brightness of the day. Though it was chilly, the autumn air was dry and the sky clear. She pushed her wiry curls beneath the base of her helmet, then fastened the strap under her chin. From all accounts, it was a typical Irish autumnal morning, crisp enough to fasten the buttons of her jacket as high as they would go to garner some extra warmth. Before moving her scooter onto the main road, she took the opportunity to study her map a final time.

She would travel along the main roads that snaked across the county, bringing her into Ennis before curving northeast toward Feakle. This was quite a distance, taking her around an hour and a half, maybe more. Had she known the county better, she may have settled on a shortcut, but sticking to the main route would be her safest bet. As she turned out onto the road, the rush of cold air hinted that this journey might be anything but comfortable.

No more than a couple of miles into her travels, face numb from the chilly wind, she groaned to herself, wishing she'd taken Gus up on his offer to accompany her. After all she'd heard about Biddy, a visit to her house alone left her feeling a little anxious. She pressed on, convinced that, if she even pulled over to reflect, she might lose her nerve.

With each passing mile, the calm beauty of County Clare unfolded. There were few other people out on the road so early, giving her an unspoiled view of the lush green countryside, with hints of Fall change everywhere. As she sped along the winding roads, the world surrounding her seemed to tick by at a slower pace. Animals grazed in the beautiful patchwork of wide-open fields, their freedom only hindered by the dry-stone walls that bordered the roads. When she moved through Ennis, that feeling of time crawling remained. The narrow streets were framed by bright-painted storefronts—remnants of the town's long market history.

As she crossed a bridge over the River Fergus, she peered into its muddy waters, swollen from recent rains, which reminded her of a stream of milk chocolate, and that set her thinking of the small pastries and thermos of hot tea she'd packed in her satchel for the journey. With a clear schedule in mind, she had not planned to stop so soon, but the chill of the morning air convinced her otherwise. And her fuel gauge provided another reason to deviate from her original strategy.

A block or two from the edge of town, she pulled in at a filling station. She unfastened her satchel from the seat and allowed the wizened attendant to set to work refueling her scooter. Her hands were frigid cold, and she fumbled to unzip the bag enough to grab out her wallet. After paying, she moved the scooter to the side of the building to shelter from the light breeze, and took out the bright-red thermos. With her fingers well chilled, it took real effort not to spill the hot liquid as she poured it into the small cup, but it was worth it when she held it in both hands, savoring the heat seeping into her flesh. Each sip sent warmth streaming through her chest, easing the knowledge that she still had the second half of the journey to go. After finishing off one of the pastries and two cups of tea, she cleaned the cup with a serviette and replaced the items in her satchel, saving what was left for later on.

Still cold, but better than before, she moved back onto the road and continued on her way to Feakle. Much like the first leg of her journey, villages that dotted the modern road opened up into beautiful countryside. Time warred against itself out here, with modernization struggling to mar a land suspended in the past, as though someone had pressed the proverbial pause button. That was one of the reasons she'd fallen in love with this country—its deep loyalty to the past, with layer upon layer of lives shared in the same spaces, forging a sense of connectivity that was difficult to find elsewhere.

Her thoughts wondered to Biddy Early, a lifelong Clare woman who had no doubt beheld many of these same sights. From the moment Old Gus mentioned the healer's name, she'd experienced a strange sensation—a strong pull—she couldn't put into words. As she drew closer to Feakle, the pull grew stronger, its energy filling her with trepidation. Before coming to Ireland, her entire existence had revolved around searching for something she couldn't quite grasp. Truth be told, it was by her own design. She had become comfortable with the constant search, desiring no end, for it would only lead to closure. Answers would yield expectations, and that was sufficient reason to avoid them. The curiosity of knowing the why burned in her, but the finality was too scary to see anything to a true end.

She had no earthly idea what she hoped to find at Biddy's, but the nudge from Old Gus had been enough. With the map's directions firm in her mind, she turned off a lonely road and made her way closer to the once-famed house. Just as the seanchaí had said, she passed a small farmhouse off to the left, with a low stone wall bordering the property. Not too long after, she came to a metal gate, unable to hold back a smile. Its wood frame looked weathered, making her think one solid push by a wayward lamb would topple it over. The crossbars were rusted, with one hanging on by little more than fragments of battered steel. She eased up and parked just beyond the gate, in case the farmer took a notion to open it. With the kickstand in place, she hopped off and gave her back and arms a much-needed stretch. Even with her riding gloves, her hands were frozen stiff, and she rubbed them together, then brought them to her mouth to thaw them with a few hot breaths.

It took longer than expected, but once feeling returned, she unfastened the chin strap of her helmet and tugged it off, freeing her mass of curls beneath. The rush of cool air tickled her scalp and neck, and she shuddered, cold but relieved to have her hair free.

She fastened her helmet to the handlebars and stepped out of the shadow of a tree and into the sun's rays, savoring its heat on her back. As she scanned the immediate area, she caught a hint of something sweet in the air and pulled it deep into her lungs.

A light breeze brushed the back of her head, and stray leaves swirled in a dance above overgrown foliage opposite the gate. Nestled along a hedgerow, a large ivy-covered elder tree stood guard over what looked to have once been a pathway, now partially covered with brambles and nettles. Kate worked her way along, stepping over and around thorny limbs, scanning the pathway ahead as it brought her to a short incline. She stopped, hand over heart, aware that something was drawing her forward, as if she was being guided. It was so strong, she even glanced behind to make sure she was alone. Then, when she went to move, her feet wouldn't budge, making her feel like she was standing in a vat of tar.

Her breath caught as a rush of raw emotion gripped her limbs, with goosebumps erupting everywhere, and seconds later her feet came free and she resumed her journey. The reality of the moment was almost overwhelming. This was the route to Biddy Early's cottage, and she was here, on it—a place where hundreds upon hundreds of people came to pay homage in hopes of having their troubles resolved. Back in Biddy's day, it was well known that you had to get here early to beat the long queue at her door. People would travel many miles to seek her guidance, and while her advice was always spot on, that didn't mean a resolution to one's troubles came easy. Old Gus told her that when Biddy gave instructions, they must be followed to the letter—anything less and your situation might worsen.

At the top of the hill, her feet came to an abrupt halt again but, instead of panicking, she smiled on realizing that she'd reached the intended destination. The old cottage was a ruin, though more intact than expected. Its roof was long gone, replaced by a canopy of wild foliage that had staked its claim on the space. She moved around the structure, her pace slow, easing aside branches at times to gain a better view. The interior was small—just one room—and most of the thick walls still stood, though years of dereliction showed everywhere. A thick wooden beam lay across the doorframe, with flecks of green paint visible here and there.

While Biddy had been a famous woman in her day, she was not without her critics. She had not always seen eye to eye with the clergy, who deemed her skill as a bean-feasa nothing short of witchcraft. This mix of sentiment carried on long after her death, as rumors spread that her cottage would bring bad luck to anyone who owned it.

The fact that this place—once legendary across the country—was just a stone's throw from the road, came as something of a surprise. No doubt, many people had passed by unaware of its existence or the prominence it once held in the area.

She took a moment to soak in the quiet solitude of the place before moving along, winding in and out of the stray branches and vines, then stopping again to breathe in the essence of the old relic. There was a certain humility about standing on a property where Biddy had lived out her days. If any stock could be put in the stories still shared, it was easy to see that she had been revered as both a strong and a wise woman. Trinkets were scattered about, on the ground, tied to branches, or placed in gaps in the walls, left as offerings to the famed bean-feasa, but there were no signs of vandalism. It was clear that people put a lot of belief in the stories of misfortune that would befall those who disrespected this place.

Her heart flipped when the stillness was broken by the snap of a twig and rustle of branches off in the distance. She pressed her hand to her chest, telling herself it was nothing but the wind in the hedgerow, though it sounded like a clap of thunder within the tranquility of this ruin. Even so, she stood motionless, scanning the area left to right, trying to pinpoint the origins of the noise. Other than a few swooping birds above, she was alone.

She pulled in a ragged breath in a futile attempt to calm her nerves, and turned back to the doorway. Sunlight flickered through the canopy, illuminating something on the ground, and she stepped forward, grasping the splintered remains of the wooden doorframe to steady herself. She squinted to make out the small object, awestruck on realizing that it was a small blue bottle, lying there on a pillow of ochre leaves. How had she missed it? She'd surveyed this area not more than a minute ago and no such bottle had been there. Or had it?

It showed no signs of being weathered by age, looking as though it had been plucked off a store shelf this morning. Perhaps it, like so many of the other offerings scattered about the cottage, had been left as a token for Biddy.

A rush of cold air pushed against her back, and she became aware of a gravitational pull drawing her hand toward the bottle. With Old Gus's warning never to disturb anything not of the earth reverberating through her mind, the last thing she wanted was to touch it.

Among her list of skills, Biddy was an accomplished herbalist. Her remedies for both people and animals were invaluable for folk who had little to offer her in return. It wasn't surprising that her sight extended to the Good People. They were the elemental—the soul of the natural world—existing on a plane that layered upon that of their human counterparts. Though worlds apart, they shared the same space, and Biddy understood this well. Her own spirit infused with the earth, and the veil of the two worlds became threadbare. She had no blinders, seeing both worlds simultaneously.

Kate pushed the seanchaí's voice to the back of her mind and crouched, bathing the bottle in her shadow. Despite his warnings, she couldn't help herself and reached for the smooth glass. She had to show it to Gus. The moment she touched it, she was struck by a great force, like a violent tempest on a raging sea. It thrust her to the ground, her eyelids clenched tight, and dragged her into utter darkness. As she clawed at the dirt, struggling to extricate herself from the vortex, images came at her in a rapid sequence—flashes of light, like flames to paper—so fast, her mind couldn't process it.

Next moment, she lurched to a standstill, facing a clearing in the woods, somewhere too far away to recognize. At its center stood a white hawthorn tree, with three crude wooden crosses thrusting out of the earth at the base of its trunk. The low hum of white noise made her want to clutch at her ears to make it stop, and she scanned the empty space for its source. Her focus was drawn to a patch of haze that began to sway, like a swarm of tiny insects in some mating dance. The shape became more opaque, with flickers of light glistening on its edges, until it took on a solid form and the haze became a full-color image—the outline of a man—its finite details manifesting one by one.

Her mouth fell open at the sight before her. Perched all alone upon a log sat Finn, more youthful than the man she knew, his face softer but the sadness in his eyes so deep her own heart stung.

A sudden flash, like bolts of light coming right at her, made her cower. She clenched her eyes tighter until it faded, then realized she was somewhere different, not because the scenery had changed but because the dark energy pressing on her had lifted. Blinking the darkness away, she scanned this new place, looking for telltale markers but nothing looked familiar. Nothing except for him.

His gray eyes looked softer, but were still tarnished by all the dreariness of the world. He sprang to his feet as a shadow crossed the lush green of the grassy clearing. The woman approached him, cloaked in a humble dress of deep-brown fabric. His eyes lit up at the sight of her. Even lost in this hazy dream, Kate couldn't deny the sting of jealousy bubbling like a witch's brew in the pit of her stomach. Tumbles of copper locks draped across the woman's shoulders, and though Kate could not see her face, there was no doubt she was beautiful. The way Finn's eyes gleamed back at her was proof enough.

A loud ringing filled her ears, like the high pitch of church bells. She watched as their mouths moved, like two players in a silent movie, the ringing drowning out their words. It only lasted a few seconds, though it felt like an eternity. The woman turned away from Finn, leaving his once-bright eyes devoid of life. All the vivid colors of the wood weakened and he stood in a dusky shadow before the scene faded to the darkest night.

In a flash, that chapter ended, replaced by the old stone façade of Cahermann House. Kate faced the front entrance as the walls began to crumble away. One by one, the bricks plummeted to the ground, sucked in by the earth until all that remained was a cloud of thick gray dust. The air shifted and, with a mighty blow, all the particles floated off into the atmosphere like the embers rising from a hearth. Her eyelids fluttered, as if she were prisoner to the deepest sleep but knew she needed to wake. The house was gone, replaced by an ancient circular stack of stones. It was a fort—a fairy fort, as Old Gus or Seán would call it. Melodious music, light on the wind, beckoned her to come closer. She tried to move but couldn't, her legs as heavy as iron, and fighting against whatever force kept her there made no difference. Frustrated, she looked at the ring of stones, hoping to see where the beautiful music might be emanating. A pale flicker of light, like a tiny firefly, moved just beyond the opening. With all the strength she could harness, she pulled her left foot free of its invisible binding, but then the gravel driveway shifted beneath her shoe. The flash of light began to grow, a thousand times more brilliant, and she raised her hand to shield her eyes from the blinding rays.

The visual came into focus with such precision she could almost see the tiny flecks of gold glimmering back. His gray eyes were no more, replaced by a radiant blue. He stared at her, and though she was still aware at the edges of her mind that it was just a vision, it felt so real. Finn stood there in the stones circle's entrance, like a guardian to another world. The music still played in the distance, and though he spoke no words, she could feel his question.

She looked down to her feet to see two black hands snaking their way up her ankles, their gnarled fingers gripping her before pulling at her, as if trying to draw her into the earth. In her panic, she looked up. Finn's eyes were still bright and clear, his face conveying utter peace—the promise of release from everything the black hands represented. If only she could move, take one step in his direction, she could be free of the darkness she was sinking into. Finn was both the question and the answer, but it was she who had to move.

As she sank further, she gripped her leg with such ferocity, she could almost feel the tips of her fingers tearing into her skin. She couldn't let the earth swallow her up. Doubling down on her efforts, she pulled, until a sudden shift in pressure saw one leg come free from the hand's devilish grasp. As she drew her foot up, the hand shrank back into the earth like a dying root, the soil closing over its hasty retreat. She repeated the process with her other leg, pulling with even more effort, but just as the ground loosened beneath her, everything went black.

Chapter Twenty

Kate awoke with a sudden jolt of cold air. She blinked several times, realizing she was lying on her side, her face nestled on a cushion of decaying leaves and damp moss. When she looked up to the canopy of vines and branches, she couldn't discern whether daylight was fading or the morning sun had been swept behind a mass of gray clouds. How long had she been asleep? She got to her feet and shook bits of leaves and dirt from her hair and face, then brushed herself down, feeling as though she were covered in detritus from head to toe.

For a long moment she stood in a daze, peering around the ruin's dim interior, as if looking for something, though she couldn't figure what. Then flashes of the visions flooded her mind, and a shiver ran across her shoulders when she remembered the blue bottle. She backed up a few paces, scanning the ground, but saw nothing but dead leaves and mossy soil. Even when she bent and raked through the earthy carpet, the bottle wasn't there, if it had been at all.

Her heart tripped a wild beat, and when she straightened to her full height, everything shifted and she swayed with dizziness. She had to get out of here. If she was as unwell as she felt, then being stuck in a dilapidated cottage most people didn't know existed was not a wise choice. She scrambled back through the doorway and pulled in a heavy breath. The air outside was different, not nearly as stagnant and heavy, and it only took a few breaths before her dizziness eased. Feeling close to her usual self again, she headed for the pathway. As she studied the sky, it was clear the daylight was indeed fading. Somehow, she had lost the better part of the day. Her legs felt about as firm as gelatin, and all she could hope was that she remained well enough to make the journey back to Doolin.

As she progressed down the short hill toward the elder tree, she kept her pace strong and her steps deliberate, and was close to running when her feet hit the roadway.

The sight of someone standing next to her scooter nearly scared her out of her skin.

"G-Gus?" she squeaked, her heart thundering like stampeding horses.

A small green car was parked a few yards beyond her scooter. In all the time she'd known him, she had never actually seen him drive a car. No doubt it was his, with the colour matching all his forest-green tweed jackets. The man clearly had a soft spot for that shade.

"What on earth? I mean, how on earth? I mean…"

"The only person you are unpredictable to is yourself, Miss McCarthy. I knew you would come out here. Why? Because you do everything you are advised not to do. That is the whole reason I suggested it in the first place." He coughed into his hand. "We will say nothing about me missing tonight's session."

She groaned inside and crossed the road, regarding him with suspicion. He was such a smart man—so in tune with the natural wiring of people—one could almost think it a shame he had settled for this rural lifestyle. With his understanding of people, he could have been a renowned psychologist, though as a seanchaí, he had achieved the same notoriety, but on his own terms. The way he told a story was a simple cover for advising lost souls in the right direction. Old Gus didn't need a fancy office with the trademark therapist's couch to do his work—he could do it just as effectively undetected.

"Now, tell me,"—his voice snapped her attention back to his curious face—"did Biddy have the answers you sought?"

She glanced back to the hidden trail across the road, still trying to decipher what the hell had happened to the past few hours, let alone derive some sort of meaning from the whole mess. There had to be a logical explanation to how she'd managed to touch a blue bottle that wasn't actually there, then spend the day napping on a pile of dead leaves and dirt inside a ruined cottage. For once, nothing creative came to mind, so she settled for the truth.

"I have no idea what happened to me," she said after a hard swallow. "All I know is something...occurred back there."

Old Gus glanced up at the sky, biting at the corner of his lower lip. "It pains me to say this, but we should get back. Night will fall before we reach Doolin, and I don't like the idea of you riding around on this deathtrap in the dark." He nodded at her scooter with clear disdain. "It is the protective old man in me. What do you say that I treat you to a nice hot cup of tea at the pub, and you can tell me all about it?"

"Fair enough," she said, not opposed to the extra time to collect her thoughts.

Old Gus followed behind her all the way back to Doolin, and it was the first time in a good while she'd felt obligated to mind the speed limit. It was already dark when she turned into the parking lot of Doonagore House, and she waited as he drove into one of the empty spots.

Fiddle music filtered through the air as she walked up to the door, and she didn't think the pub would be quiet enough for a good chat, but this wasn't a conversation she wanted overheard. Inside, she waved to James behind the bar, and he responded with a surprised grin at the sight of Old Gus at her side. Come tomorrow, she supposed he would have some joke about the seanchaí being her suitor, but she didn't really care at that moment.

As luck would have it, Old Gus's favorite snug was available in the corner, and she took a seat while he set about getting their tea. She wondered how many twenty-four-year-olds could boast of sipping a cup of tea in a pub on a Friday night with a man old enough to be their granddad.

The seanchaí took his seat, dropped two spoonfuls of brown sugar into his cup, and stirred the dark brew with what Kate considered great patience. The suspense had to be killing him, but she let the silence between them linger a bit longer.

When his tea was prepared just as he liked it, he held it to his lips, raising a prompting eyebrow at her.

She glanced about, then leaned closer. "Finn told me of a blue bottle he gave to Biddy Early. The very one you spoke of."

"I have heard tell of the blue bottle for many years," he said with a smile. "There are a good many people who think it was all just legend, but I always believed it to be true."

"Honestly, I didn't at first. I thought for sure it was all just folklore and fables. That was until I touched it myself."

Old Gus lowered his cup to the saucer, his gaze never leaving her face.

"It showed me things, Gus. Things I cannot quite understand."

"It was Biddy who showed those things to you. I am as sure of it as I sit here and breathe. Just what did it show you, Miss McCarthy? We must follow what she says down to the letter."

"Do you remember a story you shared once? About the farmer in Sligo? He had spit out a curse on the land?"

"He spat out a curse on the Good People," Old Gus added.

"I know this sounds absolutely crazy coming from my lips, of all people, but I know that story is true. When Finn told me of his past, it was almost word for word, except for one detail—the girl he fell in love with wasn't the farmer's daughter, it was Biddy. At first, I was skeptical. I thought he might be lying, just telling me some old tale he didn't think I knew. Today, when I touched the bottle, I saw everything, down to the last detail. Finn is the fairy from that story."

She went on to recount the tale Finn had told her, and shared everything that happened in Biddy's cottage. One by one, she spilled out every detail.

"That makes perfect sense to me," the seanchaí said. "You see, the fairy's name was indeed Finnley. The fair-haired hero, they called him. Tell me, Kate, did Finn ever tell you his name?"

She tilted her head, remembering the first night they'd met, then let out a soft chuckle. "No. Now that I recall, it was embossed on his horse's saddle. I guessed it was his, though I thought at the time it could have been the horse's."

"A fairy will never tell you their name. It is a tell-tale sign." He turned his cup, tapping his forefinger on its rim. "You see, there are two types of fairies: Ones who bring good into the world, and ones who bring hardships onto the people. Your Finnley was meant to be the good sort, but the bitterness he felt in his heart for the farmer unbalanced his world. As the story goes, the farmer, seeing the error of his ways, released him from the curse, but he wasn't free. The Good People have their own forms of justice."

"Yes, he told me that."

"Finn could never be free until he made it right with his own kind. That's why he could never go back. He had to settle up for the imbalance his hatred created." He took another sip of his tea, smacking his lips as he set the cup back on its saucer. "He was sentenced to wander the earth until he found love. The truest form of heart that would set his soul free at last. I never heard that he'd met Biddy Early, but I cannot discount that it happened. You see, Biddy was precisely the kind of person who could have helped him. She could see both worlds very clearly. And she would have known that the woe he created in the human world could only be settled by finding love in the same place."

"I guess I wasn't paying as much attention as I should have been," Kate said, closing her eyes for a moment and grimacing. "Typical of me."

"If memory serves me correctly, I never did get a chance to finish that story that night."

"No, that was the time I found the comb on the floor." She pointed to the spot. "If only I'd heeded your warning."

"And what if you had known? Could you have stopped it? If your Finn couldn't, what makes you think you could?"

"I would have done anything in the world to save my parents."

"Aye, but when the banshee foretells death, there is nothing can be changed. If it is not today, it will be tomorrow. You are powerless to change the way things are meant to be. You cannot change the tide, my dear, it comes whether you want it to or not."

She nodded at that, releasing a breath through puffed cheeks. "If I am the one Finn has been looking for, the one Biddy foretold of, then why isn't this easy? He betrayed me. He could have told me the truth so many times."

"I admit he could have been a bit more forthcoming, but to what end? Would you have believed him in the beginning? If you hadn't seen the truth for yourself, would you believe him now?"

"Probably not," she said, rolling her eyes. She pinched the bridge of her nose. "For all his failings in the honesty department, I can't seem to shake him out of my heart."

"Little do we realize that the true love we spend our whole lives trying to find is the same one people have sought since time began. Some things are just timeless. All those emotions are just too much to resist. Everyone wants the love story that never ends, the feeling only the anticipation of a first kiss can give. At our core, no matter how reluctant we are to admit it, we are all hopeless romantics."

She shifted on her seat. "I hate this. What possible future could we have together? Why can't we just go on as we were before? Nothing really has to change."

"Haven't you ever wondered why your suitor only appears to you? You have never run into him on a Saturday afternoon in the village, have you? Why has he never been inclined to visit the pub? I imagine the rest of us would be quite amused to see you deliver a freshly poured pint to an empty booth. You are the only one who can see your Finnley, my dear. Magic, as splendid as it is, still has its limitations. You can be part of his world, but he can never fully be part of yours."

"So, the two of us getting a flat together and Finn picking up a job at the local hardware store is out of the question?"

"I am afraid it isn't very logical." The smile in Old Gus's eyes made her think he might have a better handle on what she should do than she did. "You have two choices, but both come with sacrifice. If you love him, you must be willing to leave this world behind, so he can finally go back to his. He has been here far too long already, and he can't remain forever. He only did so to find his true happiness. Now that he's found you, there is a balance that must be restored. If you stay here, continue on with your own life, then you must leave him entirely. It is only fair to Finn. He must go home. There is no other way."

Chapter Twenty-One

Kate knew what she would find when she crested that hill, but it still didn't lessen the shock. The Georgian manor house was gone, its pristine stonework erased off the earth, like it had been swept away by a wind of biblical proportions. In its place was a symmetrical stack of dry stone, formed into three circles, each one nestled inside the next—one of tens of thousands of bronze-age forts that dotted the whole of Ireland. Tall grass, its lush green drained by the chill of the coming solstice, hugged the outside perimeter. Even taller grass filled the center of the structure.

Old Gus had spoken more than once on the mystical qualities of these places. Fairy forts were still deeply revered by the local folk, and were known to hold just as much magic as they did mayhem. The Good People dwelt within these, and any human would do well not to enter uninvited. For those who were welcomed into these sacred sites, they must know it didn't come without risk. Even sheepdogs and livestock were not blind to the dangers of entering a fort that lay out in the farmer's fields, for those not of the Good People's world could find themselves trapped if the residents decided not to allow passage back out again.

Kate couldn't shake her disbelief at how real the house had seemed. She remembered walking its halls, touching the smooth oak panels that lined the walls, and smelling the varnish of centuries of care. It had felt just as alive as the field of buttercups hidden deep in Dromore Woods.

She considered all that had passed between her and Finn. How simple it would have been for him to keep her trapped. She had entered into his world time and again, unwittingly, and recalled the feel of the crushed berries oozing between her fingers that day in the woods. And there was nothing unreal about the fairy food she had eaten. Yet, never once had he made any effort to keep her against her will. On the contrary, he'd gone out of his way to ensure her safe conduct home each and every time. The man even bartered with the banshee for her safety, a woman a thousand times more powerful than he, who, if provoked, could have turned on him. Finn had spent every minute, of every hour, of every day, over the last hundred years, searching for the promised person. Somehow, he wasn't disappointed with the rotten lot he got with her. If anything, he thought every bit of her was worth the wait.

Now, as she stood there, all her hours of planning and worries about what she should do vanished because Finn stood at the entrance, with a seriousness in his eyes she could read with ease. They both knew what was being asked. She couldn't have it both ways. If she took his hand, she would leave all of this world for him, breaking free of the earth's black hands that held her planted. Finn's world was a place of peace and respite, where all the magic of nature would surround her, taking her into its tender fold, and where the only shred of darkness came when the human world touched it.

If she didn't take his hand, she would never see him again. It was a decision only she could make, and one that had to be made with the purest of heart. To enter into his world was to turn her back on her own—there would be no going back—but the reality was that she had nothing left to turn back to.

With her heart wide open, she reached out in a leap of absolute faith, accepting the silky caress of his fingers. He was hers, forever. In truth, he had always been hers. There was never meant to be a Finn without her. Even if it had taken her a lifetime to figure it out, she was sure she was meant to be here, in this time and place, her hand in his. He turned, linking her arm in his, the tall grass of the stone fort giving way to a field of golden buttercups in full bloom.

Chapter
Twenty-Two

The old seanchaí took his seat in the wooden rocking chair. Its seat's varnish had long been worn away, a legacy of the many mothers who'd lulled their babies into the wee hours of the night. At his feet, many little ones had gathered, anxious to hear tales of magic that lit their imagination, and curses that darkened the corners of their dreams. It was late in the evening, and the children, sitting wide-eyed in anticipation, should have long been tucked in their beds.

Right then, the tiny house was bursting at its seams, filled with neighbors and friends, laughter and music—the breath of life filtering through every room. A turf fire burned in the hearth, its embers glowing, as though they had no concept of time, with two fresh peat bricks filling the dwelling with their earthy sweet aroma.

Old Gus leaned forward, running his weathered palms across the tops of his thighs to rest on his knees.

"This tale is by far the best I have ever told. 'Tis a story I know to be true, as I knew the girl myself. It happened right here in County Clare."

He paused, allowing his eager audience a moment to scoot in a smidge closer.

"This is the story about the American girl who walked into the fairy fort up on Cahermann Hill… and was never seen again."

About the Author

As a child, Tasha Sheipline wanted to be a ballerina, marry a doctor, and have a pony. Since none of these dreams came to fruition, she became a teacher instead. Teaching others has proved an empowering endeavor.

An avid reader, Tasha has a long held belief that you can never have too many books. Her favorite authors include Alison Weir, William Shakespeare, Edgar Allan Poe and Jane Austin. She is certainly not opposed to sprinkling in a good Tessa Dare romance novel when time allows.

She began writing as a creative outlet, and it soon blossomed into a real passion. A lover of history, Tasha has a specific fondness for the medieval through early modern eras. She loves to infuse characters and events from these areas into her writing.

Her favorite pastimes include traveling, watching historical documentaries, and adding to her growing collection of antique books. Tasha lives in a small town in Ohio with her husband, children, and three corgi's.

Also by Tasha Sheipline

The Whisper Series:

Dark Palace

Blood in the Chapel Royal

Yorkshire Rose

County Clare